CRESCENT MARKED

StarHaven Sanctuary: Book One

Tera Lyn Cortez

Original cover art by Melony Paradise
Paradise Cover Designs

DEDICATION

For the dreamers, the readers,

and those who let the magic of words

take them to amazing and mystical new worlds.

CHAPTER ONE

The empty highway flashed outside my window as I sped by, doing ten miles over the posted speed limit. My tires flew over dry pavement in spite of the rainstorm earlier in the night, although the dark clouds overhead threatened to open up again. The green glow from the radio clock told me it was almost three in the morning.

It took me about an hour to get home during the day, but I was on track to get there in just under forty-five minutes tonight, thanks to the lack of traffic and my increased rate of travel. Had I not agreed to trade for the night shift tonight, I would have been at home for whatever emergency had cropped up, instead of my mother needing to leave a message on my cell when I didn't answer. Nine words that made my stomach drop.

The tension in my shoulders traveled up my neck and collected into a throbbing headache at the base of my skull as I navigated the road, while her message replayed itself over and over in my mind. It instantly turned my blood to ice. In a monotone voice, my mother asked me to come home as soon as I heard it. Nothing more. Her phone went straight to the answering machine when I tried to get more clarification. Why?

Signaling for the exit, I glanced at the clock again. I'd made good time and only had about ten minutes before I would be able to see what had made her leave such a cryptic sentence. I'd prayed the whole way that she hadn't had a medical emergency.

At the bottom of the ramp rainwater had pooled just before the stoplight, which remained green as I careened down the pavement. Hitting the brakes too late, I felt the tires begin to slide out from under me, shuddering as they tried to get a grip on the asphalt beneath them. The back end of the car slipped out of my control and I clenched the steering wheel as I spun in circles through the intersection. The Mountain Dew in my cup holder escaped its lid and splashed over my denim-clad legs and the front of my stereo. As my sedan came to a stop, I closed my eyes briefly, tasting the blood on my tongue, which I'd bitten in my panic, then opened them to see that the light had changed to red during my ordeal. With a shaky hand, I reached up to wipe away the sticky rivulets of soda that ran down my cheek.

Looking around for oncoming traffic, I pulled off to the side of the road and put it in park, my entire body trembling from the adrenaline. Pushing the button to put my flashers on, I leaned my forehead down to rest on the steering wheel as I attempted to regain control of my body. Every muscle attached to my five-foot-tall skeleton was pulled taut and quivering from the exertion of trying to wrangle over a ton of out-of-control steel back into submission. The smell of my burnt tires wafted in through the air vents.

Worry for my mother shortened the amount of time I was willing to sit on the shoulder, and I pushed the button to turn off my emergency lights less than five minutes after the spin out had begun. The rest of the journey would be made far more carefully than I originally set out. I didn't need to add a second trauma to what she already needed to deal with.

Making a right onto James Street, I passed through the sleeping neighborhood. Our house sat dark as I pulled into the driveway, not even the porch light on to guide me to the front door. Singling out the house key, I felt for the doorknob on the shadowed front porch. It took some scraping and maneuvering, but I managed to get the key into the keyhole and let myself in.

"Mom? Hello?"

My purse thudded down onto the wooden entry table. Keys dropped next to it, missing the vintage ceramic bowl sitting there for the purpose of catching them.

"Mom?" I called her name again, saying silent prayers it was nowhere near as serious as my overactive imagination made it out to be.

Entering the dining room, I saw her seated at the table, room dark and her phone in front of her on the woven place mat. She sat hunched over, resting her forearms against the table. Her head dropped forward, chin almost resting on her chest. I could smell the burnt coffee that had been left on the warmer too long and walked past her to turn it off.

"Thank goodness you're alright! I worried the whole way here when you didn't answer your phone. What is going on?"

She didn't lift her eyes from the tabletop. Until she spoke, I had no idea if she'd even heard me. "Leah, your Aunt Aimee has died."

"What? No. She's too young to die. There must be some mistake. What happened?" Tears welled up immediately and spilled down my cheeks.

Guilt swamped me; it had been far too long since I made it out to see her. Too long since we had been together for a real visit. I thought of the email sitting in my inbox, waiting for me to reply. It had been my last chance to communicate with her and I'd brushed it off, relegating it to the pile of things to do "later."

My aunt happened to be my mother's only sister, and my favorite person on the entire planet, in spite of the two of them not getting along very well. Growing up, I spent weeks on end with her at her property on the peninsula. My aunt was the caretaker of a huge private sanctuary for wolves, and I'd always felt at home there.

"I'll tell you what I know as we drive. The police have requested we come right away. Go pack a small bag if you want."

"Do you want me to pack a bag for you real quick?"

She shook her head. "I won't be staying. I just want to deal with whatever business they have for me and get back home."

Taking the stairs two at a time, I ran to my room and tossed a couple changes of clothes and some necessities into an overnight bag. Then I changed from my wet work jeans to clean, casual jeans and my favorite hooded sweatshirt before heading back downstairs, tennis shoes in hand.

"I'm ready." I stuffed my feet into my shoes as I looked around the room to be certain everything was off that needed to be.

Mom stood up, moving stiffly as if she'd been in that chair for a very long time. Her purse was the only item she grabbed as she headed to the front door. I grabbed her phone for her as I passed the table.

"What about a coat, or a sweatshirt at least?"

Wrinkling her forehead, she looked around as if she didn't quite understand my question before turning to the hall closet. She reached in without even looking and pulled out the first item she touched. One of my zippered jackets. I didn't attempt to suggest anything different.

"Mom, I'm so sorry. I can't imagine how hard this is for you."

She held up her hand to stop me from speaking anymore. "Thank you, but we both know Aimee and I weren't close." She paused. "I am sorry that it's too late to change that now."

The two of us piled into her car. As I buckled, I took a sideways glance at my mother. I never knew for sure what had driven the two of them apart, although I suspected the last straw had to do with the time I spent at the sanctuary. My last visit there seemed to slam the door shut between them for good.

Even at seventeen, I had loved going to visit. Something about the place called to me even when I wasn't there. On that last visit, I'd been out walking in the woods when my mother came to pick me up. The wolves tended to stay much further out in the forest, but I had always been instructed to stay close to the house just in case.

This particular walk I had gone farther than normal, and just before I reached the clearing where the house was situated, a low growl came from off to my left. The bushes snapped as the branches shivered and a pair of glowing amber eyes appeared. I'd never seen any of the animals so close to the clearing before. I gasped and stumbled backwards, losing my footing thanks to a root in the pathway.

Despite attempting to catch myself and flailing my arms to try and catch my balance, my backside landed on the dirt with a thud. My left hand hit the ground first, onto a sharp rock that tore the meaty part of my palm wide open, right over my crescent shaped birthmark. Blood poured from the wound and onto the ground. To my shock, the earth immediately absorbed it. I watched in awe as the crimson liquid ran down my hand and off my fingertips in droplets, just to disappear as they hit the dirt.

I'd all but forgotten about the wolf until movement caught my eye and I realized it had crept forward. I got to my feet, moving slowly while backing towards the clearing. My aunt's yells reached my ears as she called my name, and my mother screamed. The wolf did not advance any further, but watched me every step of the way until I reached the tree line. Then it disappeared as if it had never been there in the first place.

Walking backward to keep an eye out, just in case, I crossed the clearing with rapid footsteps. My mom herded me directly into the car to take me for stitches, yelling at my aunt the entire way. "This is your fault. I told you this would happen. You stay away from her from now on."

"It was an accident. It's not like I bled her on purpose!" my aunt answered my mother's accusations from the cover of the back porch, not trying to get close to me.

I tried to interject, and explain that it had been my own fault, but my mother wouldn't hear it. She slammed the car door closed and peeled down the gravel road leading to the highway. She never allowed me to go back for a visit again.

I shook my head, somewhat in awe of how clearly the memory had come to me, playing like a movie in my mind. In the ten years since it happened, I hadn't thought about it much. My aunt and I emailed and spoke on the phone regularly, and she had come to visit a few times, but I hadn't set foot on sanctuary property since. It had just been easier to appease my mother, and my aunt understood.

Only once did I make an effort to ask my mother what about that day made her so angry. She cut off my query with a stern reminder that her relationship with her sister was none of my concern, and I would be best served by minding my own business. The argument that it became my business when she prevented from seeing the only living member of family I had fell on deaf ears.

The sun rose as we drove, bringing daylight to the scenery around us. I tore my gaze from the landscape outside the window to glance toward my mom. Her knuckles were white on the steering wheel, her face grim. If my memory served me correctly, we should have been close to the exit we needed to take. I'd hoped to get her to open up some on the drive, but I'd gotten lost in the past and she hadn't seemed to be in the mood for conversation.

"Are you okay, Mom? Do you want me to drive the rest of the way?"

"I'm fine and no thank you," she responded without taking her eyes off the road.

Once we pulled off the freeway, my mother took a turn onto a two-lane highway. The rain that had been beating against the roof of the car finally waned. Few other vehicles traveled the road this early in the morning, and the fog made it seem as if we were the only people around. The next turn took us off the paved road and onto a gravel lane that seemed to stretch on forever.

The tires of the jeep splashed through potholes that would have swallowed a smaller car whole. Thick grayish water splashed up the sides, prompting me to shut the windows to avoid being soaked, in spite of the balmy morning air. We'd long since left the asphalt and I would have suspected my mother made a wrong turn, except this particular path had no wrong turns to make.

The turn off the main highway led onto a fairly well-maintained, though rocky, road, wide enough for two vehicles to squeak past one another if each hugged their respective side, not that I'd seen a single other car. But, as we made our way further into the forest, the road narrowed by almost imperceptible increments, until the brush lining the path began scratching along the side panels, sounding like fingernails on a chalkboard. If not for the windows being closed, the vegetation would have been reaching in and plucking at my hair and clothes with their skeletal branches.

She turned the windshield wipers up, squinting through the wave dislodged by her drive through another tiny lake in the middle of the "road." In spite of the rising sun, she'd had to turn the headlights back on long before in order to see through the gloom of the crowded trees. As we rounded a bend in the path, they illuminated the heavy wooden sign I'd been watching for, the one announcing we had reached sanctuary land and trespassers were expressly forbidden. StarHaven Sanctuary.

The scar on my hand began to ache, and a sigh escaped me before I realized it was waiting to escape. My attempt to swallow it back proved unsuccessful.

"What are you sighing about?" My mother's tone had a sharp edge to it, as if she expected me to say something unpleasant.

"Nothing, Mom. Don't worry about it."

She didn't bother to respond, and we drove the rest of the way up the winding drive in silence. As we pulled into the clearing, the house loomed above us, dark and lonely aside from the porch light. It looked abandoned already, even though Aimee had been alive and well yesterday morning when she sent me that email.

The officer stationed on the porch came down to the car and my mother explained to him who we were and why we were there. He instructed her to park the car and go around back.

"An officer will lead you to where you need to go." He tipped his hat as my mother nodded wordlessly.

As she shut off the car and rolled the window back up, she turned to me. "Why don't you wait in the house for me? You don't need to see this."

"Actually, I do, and I absolutely will not. You weren't even close to her. If anyone should go, it should be me. You're welcome to wait here if you want."

Her lips pursed, and she clenched the keys in her hand. Instant remorse for my harsh words flooded me. She opened her mouth as she began to argue with me, but she closed it again without making a sound and opened the car door. Exiting the vehicle, I stood for a moment and listened to the wind blow through the trees. The distinctive smell of wet earth greeted my nostrils.

Pushing the car door closed, I paused to take in my surroundings before moving to walk around the house as the officer had instructed. The giant evergreen trees towered above us, surrounding the clearing like immobile sentinels. No other structures stood on the property aside from my aunt's house. For some reason even the humans seemed out of place here.

A howl rose with the wind, and the hair on the back of my neck stood up. The skin on my arms puckered up into goosebumps in spite of my sweater and the scar on my hand throbbed. I rubbed it absentmindedly with my thumb, stopping short when I caught my mother staring at my hands with a frown on her lips.

I wondered if she knew more about the birthmark/scar than she had ever let on.

CHAPTER TWO

Temporary lights had been set up to illuminate the path around the house to the back, where, as promised, another officer was waiting for us. The sunrise had come and gone, but the towering trees kept the area dim for much of the day.

"I apologize for the long walk, but we don't have any ATVs here that can fit the trail. Everybody is going in and out on foot."

My mother just nodded, her expression

unchanging. I gave him a small smile. "Don't worry about it. We are familiar with the property and its quirks."

Mom's head jerked up. "You've been to the ruins before?"

My head shook from side to side. "No, but I have walked some of the other trails. The forest is thick and the trails are uneven, even in the best of spots."

She exhaled as her shoulders returned to their normal position, some of the tension gone. I caught the officer watching us out of the side of my eye and turned toward him, holding my hand out in indication that we were ready to follow his lead.

In spite of his powerful flashlight, the darkness pressed in from the trees around us. Except for the occasional gust of wind, the forest seemed to be silent. There were no birds calling out and no small animals rustling through the underbrush. Even the insects made no noise. As we walked, I kept my eyes out for any of the wolves, but they seemed to be far from the trail, well out of the vicinity where all the activity took place.

The only creatures I saw were a pair of chipmunks, perched on the lowest branch of a large pine tree right near the edge of the clearing. They watched us pass by, unmoving, yet aware of our presence. At any other time, I would have stopped to watch them, and perhaps gone to the house in search of a snack to offer in an attempt to make friends. Turning back once, I noted that they still watched us, silently making sure we continued on our way.

The only sound aside from our own breathing was our footsteps on the pine needle covered path, which were muffled by the layer of forest detritus. My awareness seemed to heighten as we approached the ruins of the old temple. The air here felt different from the rest of the woods, heavier somehow.

The decaying buildings sprang up out of the trees between one step and the next. In one moment I had nothing but trees in front of me, then I blinked and the trees disappeared, crumbling stone in their place. Aunt Aimee had told me of the site, making me aware of its existence, but had requested I stay far from it. She never explained its purpose or why I shouldn't go near it, stating only that its unsteady structure was dangerous.

In stark contrast to the failing walls and smaller buildings around it, a single structure resembling a temple stood in the center of the rubble. While covered in moss and obviously old, it appeared to be mostly intact. Columns flanked the front entrance, which didn't actually have a door, and vines had grown up around them.

Once again, the hair on the back of my neck stood up as we approached it. I could feel a darkness nearby, but couldn't put my finger on what it might be or where it came from. The unease leeched into my bones, leaving a hollow feeling.

Two officers stood near the doorway and raised a hand in greeting as we approached. They, too, appeared to be uncomfortable in the situation. More so than one might expect for a simple unattended death.

"Hello, I'm officer Stanton. I'm so very sorry for your loss. We appreciate you coming all the way out here. I'm hoping you could take a look around and tell us if anything seems off to you, or is missing, and identify the body?"

My mom bit her lip and peered past him into the dark interior. At first, I couldn't tell if she felt sad or scared. "I will try. I haven't entered this building in decades, so I don't know what all remained inside. It held nothing of monetary value, as far as I know. I can definitely identify my sister for you though."

I eyed her from off to the side. It was news to me

that she had ever been to the ruins, much less inside the temple. For a woman who had always claimed she steered clear of the sanctuary, there seemed to be a few details she had neglected to mention to me. We followed the officer inside after he handed us each a flashlight, explaining that without electricity they were unable to set up any of the bigger lights like we had seen at the house.

As we crossed the threshold I shivered. The temperature dropped by at least fifteen degrees and the cool air had an unfamiliar tinge to it. My scar began to itch. I scratched at it, doing little to ease the sensation.

The short entry hall led to a single open room that took up most of the footprint of the architecture. Pictures had been carved into the walls and statues rested on pedestals. The floor tiles each sported individual symbols that I did not recognize. In the far left corner stood a shrine of some sort. My aunt's body lay at the foot of it.

"We believe she suffered a heart attack, but obviously the official cause will come from our medical examiner's office." The officer used a gentle tone as he explained what they knew to my mom.

"Leah, please don't look," Mom said. Her eyes

remained trained on the floor as she made the request.

Intuition led me to ignore her, unable to dispel the feeling that I needed to be close to my aunt one more time. More tears spilled down my cheeks as I walked over to the raised platform, my mother and the officer right behind me. I heard my mother let out a small sound as we approached, almost as if she was choking on something.

"That's Aimee." The words were strangled as they left her throat.

She turned away; the officer taking her arm to help her as she turned away from the sight of her sister. I continued forward and knelt at my aunt's side. Her veins had turned black, running across her body like a road map. They stood out against her translucent skin.

Strangely, neither my mother nor the officer seemed to take notice of that detail. Could they really not see it? Other than that peculiar symptom, the body showed no other signs of trauma and gave no indication as to what might have been the cause of her death. Through the tears, I took in every detail I could. Instinct told me they might be important later.

Her long hair cascaded down the steps, much longer than it had been the last time we were together. I reached out to touch it gently before moving on in my visual examination. It remained soft and smooth, even in her last moments. Both eyes were closed, as was her mouth, her lips pale. Her clothing looked to be average every day wear; her style leaned to the more casual apparel.

Both her hands rested close together on her chest, clenched into fists. As I leaned over her, a tear dropped from my chin onto her hands, causing a brief blue glow to come from one of them, catching my eye. When I did a double take, it was gone. Reaching out, I touched her left hand, intending it to be a comforting gesture. The contact caused her tightly clenched fist to open, revealing an old metal skeleton key in her grip. Glancing back to be sure the officer and my mother were still occupied, I reached out and picked it up, curling my fingers around it.

The iron itself felt as if it had been laying in the snow, but the longer I held it the more feverish I became. Heat crawled up from deep in my belly, causing my cheeks to flush and beads of sweat to form along my brow. Wiping them away, I slipped the key into my pocket, immediately feeling relief once I no longer maintained contact with the artifact.

Just in case, I reached out and gently stroked her other hand with just my fingertip. Her fingers did not relax or open, and I didn't see anything clutched between them.

I stared down at her body, unable to believe that her life ended this way. Guilt for not coming to see her when I had the chance ate at me. She'd been all alone out here for years, since my uncle had disappeared when I was a very little girl, and I let my mother influence me against what I knew would have been the right thing to do.

A touch on my shoulder brought me back to the present and caused me to jump, so that I lost my balance and tumbled off the step I had been kneeling on. My right elbow caught the edge of the stone tread, sending searing pain up my arm. Aside from that, the only other thing injured was my rear end as I landed squarely on the edge of the next stair down. And my pride.

"Leah, are you alright? I'm so sorry." My mom peered down at me as she leaned over to help me up.

"It's okay, and I'm fine. I guess I was just lost in thought. I feel so guilty that she has been alone out here for all these years and I didn't make it back to visit her." I sighed. I rubbed the offending elbow. There would be a nasty bruise there by the end of the day.

The muscles in my mother's jaw clenched as she gritted her teeth. "I suppose a lot of that is my fault." Her eyes were sad as she said it.

I shook my head. "I'm an adult. Have been for a long time now. I could have come to see her if I wanted to."

The officer interrupted us. "We'd like to remove the body now, and there's no reason for you to see that. Can we escort you back to the house?"

"When will we be able to make funeral plans and lay her to rest?"

"I can't be specific for you, as all unattended deaths require an autopsy, but I can't imagine it would be a very long time. The medical examiner's office will get in touch with you once they are ready to release your sister."

My mom nodded and turned away. I reached out, touching Aunt Aimee's arm one last time. What I wanted was to hug her, and to feel her arms around me one last time, but my chance at that no longer existed. Without speaking the words aloud, I promised her that I would somehow find out what had happened to her and make it right. Doctor or not, but this didn't look like a straightforward heart attack to me.

As we moved toward the entrance to the temple, I felt as if something tried to tug me back inside. I turned around, taking a glance at the interior that was visible from where I stood. Nothing seemed obviously amiss, if you ignored my aunt's body at the base of the altar, but I knew I'd be back here soon to investigate further.

We exited the ruins back into the forest as the wind picked up and I could smell more rain on the horizon. At some point while we were inside, the emergency medical personnel arrived with a gurney to transport my aunt out of the temple. They entered once we were clear of the building, and at that exact moment a wolf howled. His call was long and mournful, rising above the treetops to greet the sun. Answering calls echoed from every direction.

The officer peered into the trees around us, visibly unnerved by the sounds. His hand rested on the butt of his gun.

My mom looked at him, eyebrows raised. "That won't be necessary. They are simply voicing their sorrow over the loss of my sister. She has been their protector for decades now."

"Besides," I interjected, "this is a sanctuary. It

would be illegal to shoot any of the wolves here."

He opened his mouth to respond, then thought better of it, and ducked his head, removing his hand and dangling it at his side instead. We followed the trail back towards my aunt's cabin with the officer leading the way.

Thunder cracked above our heads, muffled only slightly by the dense forest. I heard the rain begin to fall before I felt it. The dense canopy of trees slowed its descent to the earth and the tops of our heads. Another wolf howled, sounding much closer than before. Picking up his pace, the officer began to swivel his head from side to side, trying to keep an equal watch all the way around us.

Before we made it halfway back to the house, we were all soaked through. The rain that made it to the forest floor turned the trail into a spongy mess that not even the layer of pine needles could keep my feet from sinking into. Tiny rivers formed and ran through the roots of the towering trees. Goosebumps erupted underneath my dripping hoodie and my jeans stuck to my legs. Water squished from my shoes and socks with every step. It made me think that the sanctuary cried over my aunt's death just as I did.

As we approached the clearing, I could see the ambulance parked at the side of the house, lights still flashing. The tiny chipmunks had moved on, probably in an attempt to get somewhere dry and out of the rain. My chest tightened, but I continued walking.

Stepping out of the forest and into the clearing gave the rain a clear shot at us. The three of us picked up the pace and made a beeline for the relative safety and cover of the back porch. My mom and the officer spent a few minutes talking as I let myself into the house through the back door, somewhat surprised to see that she had left it unlocked. Not that she had many nosy neighbors who'd let themselves in.

I made my way into the kitchen, standing at the sink and staring out the window toward the forest. As I watched, the medics with the gurney exited the forest and headed toward the ambulance. They, too, were sopping wet. Part of me was thankful the black plastic body bag kept my aunt dry. The other half screamed inside that they needed to unzip and not keep her in there, that she couldn't breathe. Unable to see the whole journey from the angle of the window, I knew when they had made it into the vehicle because the flashing lights no longer reflected through the yard.

Somehow I doubted the autopsy would give us any clues to my aunt's true manner of death, but I had high hopes that the answer was somewhere within the house, and I had every intention of finding it. Whoever did this to her would not go unpunished.

CHAPTER THREE

The kitchen looked to be much the same as the last time I'd been in it. Nothing major had changed, not even the color scheme. Rummaging through the cupboards, I found the coffee and filters, putting on a fresh pot. Both Mother and I could use some, and I figured the officers would appreciate a hot cup too if they had to be stuck here much longer.

Opening the fridge, I found my aunt's favorite French vanilla creamer, right on the shelf it had always been kept. The sight brought a smile to my face. She was a creature of habit, if nothing else. When I used to come and visit, she always made me hot cocoa and added some of her creamer to my cup, just the same as she did to her own. We'd sit at the kitchen table or in front of the fireplace in the main living room and just chat, sharing thoughts and dreams with each other. She had always encouraged me, no matter what crazy things I told her I wanted to do with my life.

The back door opened and my mother made her way in. "Do I smell coffee?"

I grinned. "Yes, you do. I figured everybody out in the rain might want a cup to warm up."

"Well, the last officers just left, so we're back to it being just you and me, kid. Let's get dry and we can have a cup."

"That was quick. I guess we'll have to drink the whole pot ourselves. And I've got to grab my bag out of the car. Lucky for you I put an extra set of sweats in there, Miss I won't need a bag."

Once I brought my duffle in, we both got dried off and changed, our hair wrapped in identical towels from the bathroom down the hall. I took a minute to study her features, realizing how much alike she and Aunt Aimee looked, almost twins and only a year and a half apart in age.

Opening the cupboard, I pulled a unicorn mug from the shelf. "Would you look at this? She still has my mug in the cupboard. As a kid I never wanted to use any other one, and as I grew older it, just became a habit to reach for it. I can't believe it's survived all these years!" The familiar sight brought a gentle wave of comfort.

My mom walked over and took the mug from my hand. "Did you know she broke it once?"

I looked at her in surprise, then back at the cup which obviously was still intact. "She did?"

A faraway look came over my mom's face. "She called me in a total panic one day. She knocked it out of the cupboard when looking for something in the back of the shelf, and it shattered when it hit the counter. She spent the next few weeks searching high and low, scouring the internet for one that was its identical twin. That's the only time you wanted to go to Auntie's house for the weekend and she put you off. She feared the temper tantrum that would ensue if you couldn't have cocoa in your mug. She wanted to order two, so she had one for backup but could never find another one like it."

Laughter bubbled up. "Temper tantrum? That sounds nothing like me. I'm sure I don't know what you are speaking of. I would never..."

Her giggles escaped to match mine. We both knew that I had quite the temper when I was a girl, and if everything wasn't just so, the entire world knew of my displeasure. Luckily, I had grown out of it. Honest.

Her smile flattened out. "I should have made more of an effort to mend fences between us."

"Mom..."

She put her hand up. "No, most of our estrangement was my fault. It just never occurred to me that we wouldn't have more time. I never in a million years would have seen this coming." She stood up. "I should probably get back to the house."

"Don't go. You don't have to be back at work right away, why don't you stay here with me?"

"Why don't you come home with me instead?" she countered.

"That's a negative, Nancy. I need to be here right now, and I think you know it. Why don't you go home and get some clothes, then come back here? Just for the weekend. If you want to go home after that, I won't argue with you."

"And you'll come home with me?"

"No promises."

The set of her shoulders told me that she knew it would be pointless to argue for the moment. "Is there anything you want me to grab from the house for you?"

"Can I make you a short list?"

I rooted through the drawers and pulled out a small notepad and pen. Using the pen inscribed with the sanctuary logo, I scribbled my requests, along with where to find each item, and handed it to her, waiting while she looked it over.

"Do you plan to be here a while? This seems like a lot of stuff for just a few days."

"Well, we're the only family she had. It seems obvious that one of us needs to stay here and go through her stuff. We need to get things straightened out and decide what needs to be done. I don't know about you, but I have no clue what needs to happen after someone passes away. All this stuff can't just sit here in limbo forever." I left out my intention to look into her true cause of death, knowing my mother would dig her heels in and refuse to have any part of it, possibly refusing to stay here with me, even temporarily.

She nodded her head, seemingly lost in thought. I watched curiously as she opened her mouth and then closed it multiple times in a row, as if she couldn't decide whether to say something or not. For a moment she looked like a goldfish in a bowl. Finally, she decided to speak.

"I know your Aunt had a will, and most of this now belongs to you. I will make a call to her attorney when I get to the house. I have the information at home."

Now it was my turn to gape like a fish, mouth open in an O. I stared at her, shell-shocked. Aunt Aimee had left all of this to me? She'd had no kids of her own, but still. You never think of what will happen after someone's death when they're so young, I guess.

Shaking my head in wonder, I brought myself back to the moment at hand. "It's getting awfully late, are you sure you want to make that drive twice more today?"

"I was thinking I would drive home now and spend the afternoon and evening gathering what we need. I can spend the night at the house and then head up here bright and early tomorrow morning, if you aren't concerned about being left here all by yourself?"

My stomach jumped at the thought of being out here all alone, but I did my best not to let on that it worried me. "I'll be fine."

"I'll make a trip to the grocery store on my way

back here tomorrow, that way we won't have to head into town again."

"We shouldn't need much. Auntie always did big grocery shopping since she didn't like to leave the sanctuary often. I bet her big freezer and pantry are full."

"I'll just get the fresh items then. And I'll be back by mid-morning at the latest."

"Sounds good, Mom." I walked over and wrapped my arms around her. For a moment she stood stiffly, then relaxed and returned the hug.

My mother had never been an overly affectionate woman, but I knew that she enjoyed the contact even when she wasn't willing to initiate it. All my life it had only been the two of us and we were close as we could be, in spite of her naturally distant ways. I always suspected it had something to do with my father, but that subject didn't make for pleasant conversation, so I avoided it. He'd never been a part of my life and I certainly wasn't looking to put forth effort for someone who couldn't be bothered to meet his own daughter.

"Keep the doors locked, just in case, okay?" She raised her eyebrows at me, the signal that said she knew I would find her request ridiculous but that she wanted me to indulge her, anyway.

I laughed. "Yes, Mom. I will lock the doors just in case the woodland animals have grown thumbs, somehow figured out how to work the doorknob and try planning an invasion. I saw a pair of chipmunks out back that looked positively threatening."

She swatted me on the butt as she walked by. "Smart ass. You never know who might try to creep up here and get nosy once the word of Aimee's death becomes common knowledge around town. Gossip travels like wildfire around here. People have always had an odd fascination with this place."

That made sense. And seeing as how I hadn't even considered that angle, I agreed wholeheartedly to keep the doors locked at all times.

"Let's see if we can find Aimee's keys to the truck, just in case there is an emergency."

I walked toward the front door, memory prodding me. She had always hung her keys on the little hook by the entryway closet. Sure enough, they were right where I had expected them to be, as if she might walk through that front door at any minute to grab them.

I picked them up, holding them in my hand for a second, before turning to show my mother. "Here they are, right where she always left them."

"Okay then. I feel better knowing you have a vehicle if you need it. I am going to head out and I'll see you tomorrow morning. Please, please, please, for the love of all that is holy, do not decide to go out walking in the woods while you are here all by yourself. Promise me that or I will never be able to sleep for the worry that will never leave my mind."

"Don't worry. I have no desire to go out walking in the woods while I'm here alone. Remember, Aunt Aimee drilled the dangers into my head from the very first visit I made up here. I could fall, hit my head, break a leg, get lost, or be eaten by a wolf or bear or whatever else is out there. I'll stay in the house or on the porch if I need some fresh air."

Still she hesitated, one hand on the doorknob.

"I promise, Mom. Go, so you can get back."

Straightening her posture as if gathering her strength, she opened the door. "I'm going. See you tomorrow, Leah. I love you."

"I love you too, Mom."

I stood in the open doorway until she drove down the gravel drive, her taillights vanishing in the trees. Taking a deep breath, I inhaled the scents of the forest around me. The silence echoed in my ears. It felt strange acknowledging that I was the only human around for miles now. Only the animals that lived here would be my company, and I might never see most of them.

Closing the door behind me, and throwing the deadbolt as promised, I began wandering my way back through the house, letting the memories take over. I stopped in the doorway of the library off the entry hall, smiling when I saw "my" shelf still intact, even after all these years. My aunt had always encouraged a love of books, and would let me read just about anything I could find that I showed an interest in.

Each time I came a new book or books would be setting on my shelf, the topics running the gamut from true crime, to space exploration, to fairy tales. I walked over to them and ran my fingers along the spines. The memories brought a strange mixture of comfort and grief.

Moving on I briefly touched on every room in the house allowing the recollections of my time here to wash over me. After my impromptu tour, I settled back in the library with a fresh cup of coffee. Seated at my aunt's desk, I closed my eyes, hoping for some sort of answers to come to me. When nothing did, I began opening her drawers to look for clues, feeling slightly guilty for intruding upon her privacy, even though she was no longer with us.

In the top drawer lay a leather-bound journal. Hesitating at the intrusion, I opened it to find only a single entry, penned two days before.

"I know now that I am no longer strong enough to contain her. I am going to have to ask for help, even though doing so will cause great pain and may ruin our relationship forever. I have no other choice. An evil of that magnitude can never be allowed to break free. No matter the cost, I will prevent the chaos from being unleashed upon the rest of the world."

I stared at the words in shock. What evil? And who did she plan to ask for help? I flipped through the rest of the book just to make sure I hadn't missed something, then came back to the handwritten message. She had known she was in danger. Why hadn't she called us?

More tears slipped down my cheeks. I don't know how I would have been able to help, but I would have done anything in my power to be here with her, to assist her.

Looking for more clues, I searched the rest of the drawers. Nobody began keeping a journal and only wrote a single entry. There had to be more of them somewhere. When the library turned up nothing, I began moving through the rest of the house, on the hunt for more of the tomes. Instinct told me they would be the key to beginning to understand what secrets the sanctuary hid.

By late afternoon every room had been inspected, and I still didn't have any other journals to read. I stood in the kitchen with a snack, trying to decide whether to go upstairs to the attic or downstairs to the basement. Something indiscernible tugged me toward the attic, and I listened.

The doorway to the uppermost section of the house sat at the end of the second-floor hallway. Locked. Returning for my aunt's keys, I worked my way through them until I found one that turned the tumbler. Pushing open the door was like stepping into another building entirely. Polished floors and sheet-rocked walls changed to weathered stair treads flanked by bare plywood.

The light switch to the right of the doorway illuminated a single hanging bulb, barely chasing away enough of the gloom for me to see where I needed to step. The staircase itself was longer than most, and steeper too. I counted nineteen stairs instead of the usual thirteen. Odd.

Reaching the top, I had to go through another door. While I saw no keyhole, it didn't seem to want to open. Gripping the handle tightly, I pushed against it with my shoulder. When it didn't give, I rested for a moment, trying to come up with a plan. My hand remained on the knob which began to warm and give off a dim glow. Staring at it in shock, I yanked my hand away. The light disappeared, and the door swung open of its own accord, giving me my first look of the attic in the manor of StarHaven Sanctuary.

CHAPTER FOUR

The single fixture didn't give off much light, but I could see. It took a moment for me to orient myself in the large space. The expansive room covered what looked to be the entire footprint of the house, filled with trunks and crates, old wardrobes and boxes of all shapes and sizes. Aside from being clean, it looked as if it sat undisturbed for years. Where did I start? How would I know where to look for journals, or anything else that might help me gain the knowledge I desired?

To take it all in, I turned in a slow circle, looking for

the additions that appeared to be the most recent. The silence in the attic unnerved me a little, causing me to shiver in spite of it not being at all chilly. The pile nearest the door seemed like the most reasonable place to start, so I pulled the flaps of a box open and peeked inside. Old clothes. I lifted out a few items, mostly sweaters and scarves, obviously moved out of the way to make room for summer items. Returning them, I moved on to the next.

I'd been at it for an hour before I ran across boxes that began to look promising. They were full of dozens of handwritten journals. Some of them were plain spiral bound notebooks like you would find in the school supplies section. Others...

Excited, I lifted the one off the top of the pile, running my hands over the pebbled leather and tracing the outline of the moon embossed onto the center of the front cover. The darkly branded image called to me. Shifting to cross my legs and relieve some of the pressure on my knees, I settled the book in my lap and pulled the smooth ribbon keeping the covers closed.

Unfamiliar handwriting covered the pages. For a moment my eyes ran over the clusters of symbols, their meaning escaping me. As I focused on the pages, the marks slowly began to make sense. Whatever language this book was written in made sense to my brain, even if I didn't realize it at first.

I read the stories that had been penned upon the pages with growing interest. Who had written them? Many of them seemed to be centered here at the sanctuary, and included the ruins, the stream and a mountain cave. The peninsula that the sanctuary sat on covered many acres of land, and the only mountain I knew of sat in the North-East corner. Near its peak cascaded the waterfall that served as the origin of the stream that ran the width of the peninsula, emptying into the sea at the other side.

Interspersed among the stories were recipes, poetry, and what looked to be... spells? I set the first volume aside and began pulling out others. At the very bottom of the box lay an old, leather-bound volume. Its cover had no title or author, just an intricately ornate moon branded into the center. My fingers traced this one as well, noting the similarities and differences between the two symbols. It seemed most of the volumes had a moon somewhere.

Careful not to break the almost three-inch spine, I inspected the first page. Reign Family Grimoire, it read.

Reign was our last name. I had my mother's maiden name, as she and my father never married. His name didn't even appear on my birth certificate. Sometimes I wondered if she had even known it, or whether they came together in a single instance, never to make contact again.

Every letter, or symbol, between the covers had been penned by hand. As I turned the pages, it became obvious that more than one person had contributed to the information on the old paper. The ink changed color, some pages faded but not difficult to read, as if preserved somehow. The size of penmanship varied, as did the slant of the letters.

No matter the writing, whether symbol or alphabet, my eyes easily relayed the information to my brain, allowing me to comprehend the message. Coming to a section titled "Beginner Spells" I paused, tempted to try them out for myself. What could it hurt? Likely nothing would come of it, and I would be laughing at myself for believing in such nonsense momentarily.

Settling on instructions to create "light to see by," I read the words through top to bottom before attempting to repeat them. Extending my left hand, palm up, as the instructions said to, I recited the words from the page, pronouncing them as best I could. Nothing. I read over them once more and tried again. Still nothing.

My hand dropped, slapping my palm onto my thigh, frustrated and a little disappointed in myself. I hadn't exactly expected anything to happen, but still. Once more I read the page through, in my mind, mouthing the words as I went along.

Something clicked, and as I read I was able to *hear* the words in my head, just like I would if someone sat beside me teaching me the correct pronunciation. Ready to give it one last try, I extended my hand once more and recited the words. In the palm of my hand a tiny orb appeared, throwing off a soft white light that illuminated most of the attic space around me. I yanked my hand back, yelping as if I had touched something hot. The glowing ball continued to float there in midair, undaunted by my freak out.

"Well, I'll be damned."

The brighter light illuminated much of the attic that hadn't been reached by the fixture hanging from the ceiling. As I scanned the room, I saw a reflection in a far corner. Perched on an eve in the attic sat a pair of chipmunks. They didn't move as we stared at each other. After a moment one of the two let out a string of chatter and they both turned and disappeared into one of the few shadows that remained in spite of the added light.

The small orb in front of me once again became the focus of my attention. My hand trembled as I reached out with my pointer finger, attempting to touch the light, in spite of knowing there would be nothing physical there. Returning my gaze to the page, I spoke the single word out loud to extinguish the light, giggling as it winked out of existence. The spell worked, and I could do magic.

I reignited my personal light source with a grin. My cheeks hurt from the width of the smile on my face. After flipping through the pages just to see what they contained, I started from the beginning and began attempting some of the other spells. Some I easily mastered, others never came to fruition. Thankful for my excellent recall ability, I committed as many of them to memory as possible, deciding it would be good to have them available, should I ever want to use them. I couldn't carry all these books with me everywhere I went.

Oh, how I wished I'd been raised here. My aunt

undoubtedly could have taught me much of this from the very beginning. By this point in my life, I could have mastered many of these skills instead of being in magical preschool with only myself as the teacher. Myself and a number of very thick textbooks.

Hours passed as I began my self-taught journey into the world of magic. After attempting a difficult spell, fatigue crept into my brain. Before I could acknowledge that it might be time to take a break, my body decided for me and everything went black.

My eyes protested as I opened them, and a tender spot throbbed at my temple where my skull made contact with the floor. The lack of windows gave me no way of knowing how many hours had passed until I heard my mom calling my name from below.

"Leah? Leah! Where are you?"

I clambered up from my spot on the floor, sending the room back into darkness as I headed for the stairs. My legs, numb and weak from being on the hard floor for so long, buckled under me, sending me sprawling across the wooden planks. A two-inch sliver embedded itself into my right forearm, just below the elbow.

"Damn it." That was going to take some finesse to get out without ripping a chunk of skin out with it.

Getting back to my feet, albeit more carefully this time, I picked up the grimoire from where it had gone flying and called out as I headed down the stairs. "Up here, Mom. Be right down."

Hobbling on my aching legs, holding the book in my left arm to avoid bleeding on it, I traversed the stairs with my right hand skimming the wall for support and met my mother in the upstairs hallway. We came face to face as I closed the attic door behind me.

"What on Earth?" Between her puckered brows and slack jaw, I gathered I must have been quite the sight.

"Long story. Before we get into it, can you help me remove this splinter?" I held my arm up for her inspection.

"You mean that twig in your arm? I certainly can, but it's not going to be a pleasant experience. I'm going to have to cut it out."

My shoulders sagged. "I was afraid you were going to say that." Pain and I had never been the best of friends.

She led me to the downstairs bathroom, rooting in the cupboards and drawers for first aid supplies. Hissing as the sting of peroxide washed over the injury, I tried to take my mind off it by telling her what I had found.

By the time she had finished playing nurse to my injuries, I'd riled her up with all of my talk about magic and spells.

"You are being ridiculous, Leah. There is no such thing as magic. You sound just like Aimee when she was younger. Always going on about spells and magic. No amount of sensible talk could convince her it didn't exist. Strange things might happen in this world, things we don't understand right away, but that doesn't mean there isn't a reasonable explanation for them."

Sighing, I thrust the book in her direction. "Okay, so what is all this written here on these pages?"

She studied them for a moment. "I have no idea what language that is, so I couldn't even begin to guess."

"I *can* read them, Mom. They're spells. Some of them, at least. Some of them are stories, meant to teach lessons, I think."

Lips pursed, she eyed me with her eyebrows raised. "Seriously? Aren't you a little too old to be playing these games? How hard did you hit your head when you fell?" She focused on the scrape at my temple, reaching out with a new cotton ball soaked in more peroxide.

My say-so would not be enough to convince her. She needed to see it with her own eyes.

Flipping to the first spell that had worked for me, I asked her to shut off the light. She sighed, but did as requested. Left hand held out with my palm facing up, I double checked the spell before reading it once more.

The little orb popped back into existence with no hesitation. My mother stared at it for a full minute, before reaching out and attempting to touch it, just as I had. She tried to pop it, as if she were popping a bubble, and let out a little hum when nothing happened. She tapped her finger against her lips, but said nothing.

I spoke the word to turn it off. "Well? Do you believe me now?"

"Aimee always was a little strange, and claimed to be able to do weird things, but she never once showed me any proof. This... This is something else."

She pursed her lips, seeming to be looking for the best way to articulate her feelings. Instead of filling the silence, I just let her think. While she appeared to be surprised, it didn't seem like the situation struck her as out of the realm of possibilities. That in itself made me wonder if she knew more than she let on so far.

"I think," she began slowly, as if testing the words, "that we need to get you away from the sanctuary and go home."

"What? No! That's not what we need to do at all, and I think you know it. Aunt Aimee was a witch of some sort, and I think we know now that I am too, or I could be at least. I need to learn more, not run away. Something isn't right about the way she died. We both know she didn't just walk all the way out to that temple for a morning stroll and drop dead of a heart attack." I paused with a deep breath in. "I just don't understand why she never taught me any of this."

Mom met my question with silence, staring off into space. The muscle in her jaw clenched and relaxed as I watched, waiting for a response. When she finally began to speak I thought she might give me some answers.

But all she said was, "I don't know."

Disappointment spread through me, but I decided to let it drop for now. We spent the rest of the day going through some of Aunt Aimee's things. Mom told stories about photos we came across from when the two of them were younger. Darkness fell, and Mom went to bed early, claiming fatigue.

With the grimoire in hand, I headed to the main room to continue reading for as long as my eyes could stand it. When the words finally began to run together, making it impossible to glean anything more from them,

I closed the book and accepted that any more reading would have to wait until the next day, after I got some sleep.

As tired as my eyes might have been, the rest of my body wasn't quite ready to quit for the night, even though I'd not slept the night before, unless you counted the time I spent passed out on the attic floor.

For a compromise, I took some cocoa out onto the back porch to relax, pondering my next steps. The moonlight illuminated the clearing, creating a stark line where the trees began. Somewhere in the not too far off distance, a wolf howled.

The temptation to walk out and look for the creature doing the howling gripped me.

CHAPTER FIVE

The sound both scared me and excited me. The metal porch swing creaked as my feet pushed back and forth, waiting for the sound to come again. My patience was rewarded with another howl, this one seeming to be much closer, and more intense. Something about it called to me, almost demanded my attention.

Standing, I stepped to the edge of the porch, wanting for some reason to walk down the stairs and follow the path into the dark woods. Fighting the urge, my eyes remained focused on the forest, wondering if the wolf would continue moving closer. A twig snapped, just past where the moonlight touched, causing me to take a step back.

Once more a howl filled the air, and this time the request was unmistakable. This wolf wanted me to come into the woods, but why? The urge to return to the house might have been strong, but my curiosity was stronger. Self-preservation apparently wasn't my strong suit. Plus, Aunt Aimee had never mentioned trouble with the wolves in all the years she'd lived here, and something lurked at the back of my mind, telling me it would be safe to answer the call.

Moving cautiously, and hoping my mother didn't wake up and catch me heading into the trees at night, my slippered feet carried me across the clearing. Pausing for just a moment to let my eyes adjust, I moved up the path, guided by instinct. Rounding a bend on the trail less than fifteen yards from the clearing brought me face to face with a huge dark gray wolf.

It sat on its haunches, motionless, staring at me with wide amber eyes. Startled, but for some reason unafraid, I met its gaze. The connection between us formed with a sizzle, sending little arcs of electricity down my spine. Never before had I experienced anything like what happened as I stood in the middle of the dark trail that night. In that moment the wolf went from being a regular forest creature, to something much, much more.

"Hello. You're Leah, right? My name is Isaiah, and I am the alpha of the StarHaven pack. Welcome to the sanctuary. I'm so sorry about your aunt, but I am very glad you're here."

His deep voice resonated through my head, not needing my ears in order to be heard. The sensation caught me off guard for a moment.

"How do you know who I am? And how can I hear you? I mean, I understand you, even though I know that wolves can't talk. Or speak English. I-" Stopping once my stuttering reached my own ears, I felt the blood rush to my cheeks, thankful for the darkness. How embarrassing.

"I knew Aimee, and she talked about you often. She, too, had the ability to communicate with the pack and spent time amongst us. Also, you bear the Mark., which all of the wolves residing in the sanctuary are aware of. The entire pack knows who you are. And, as the alpha, your crescent moon calls to me. Do you remember the day you last came to walk in the woods, when you fell and cut yourself? The moment your blood spilled onto the earth you were accepted as an ally of the sanctuary."

"You... That was you, that day?" Looking back, she wondered why she hadn't recognized those eyes immediately.

"That was the day your Mark was activated. But I wasn't the alpha then and couldn't make the connection with you like I did just now. It requires a certain amount of power, and I just wasn't strong enough. That, and we didn't have much time in the moment. I think I may have frightened you, and I'm sorry."

"But, how do you know these things? Do you know why Aunt Aimee didn't tell me about you, or teach me her magic? She just let me leave and never tried to tell me about her powers, or the sanctuary, or anything else!" Frustration rang in my voice, but I couldn't help it.

"I don't have the answers you are seeking. I never questioned why Aimee made the decisions she did. She may have mentioned it at some point, but..." He paused for a beat before continuing. "Unfortunately, part of the curse upon our land makes our memories foggy and we have trouble remembering things that we should. There is a legend tied to the origin of the Crescent Mark, and those few who receive it, but the specifics escape me." His voice died off, as if he needed to expend more energy to finish his thoughts. "I do know your aunt has old books, and your family grimoires, that will begin to teach you the things you need to know."

For a moment I debated how much to tell him about what I had already been up to in my short time here. Instinct told me that I could be open with him, and that he was trustworthy. Yet something held me back. Perhaps the unnatural attraction creeping its way through my core. The pull toward him was so strong already.

"I've already found some of her books in the attic. I found them while searching for clues about how she might have died, and I can follow some of the spells and do a little magic. Nothing impressive yet, though." My sigh conveyed my disappointment. "I've barely just discovered these things are possible, and I wish that I had a better teacher than myself. I've lost so much time and potential by not knowing it existed."

"Then you already have a good start. I think you will do fine. We need you, Leah. The pack and the sanctuary itself needs you. You are special, and we need your help to contain the evil, before it spreads and destroys us all."

I sighed. Vanquishing evil sounded like it might be a bit above my station in life for the time being. I'd rather satisfy my curiosity. "Tell me more about yourself, and the pack, and the sanctuary. If you don't mind, that is. There is so much I want to know, and I'm afraid to wait too long to ask my questions now, because I know that time is fleeting. I just keep thinking of all the questions I could have asked Aunt Aimee, if I had just come to visit her like I'd been thinking of doing. But stupid shit just kept getting in the way, and now I will never have the chance again." A tear welled up and slid down my cheek, hot against my skin in the cool night air.

"I'm sorry. I know how it feels to lose someone too soon. My mom died when I was just a baby. My father raised me alone, with the help of the pack, of course. Then he died, too. Right before you saw me in the woods that day, maybe two weeks before? The curse blurs even that from my memory. It makes it so there isn't much I can share with you that you might find useful."

"I'm so sorry. I didn't mean to have you tell me only the sad things."

Isaiah shook his furry head. "Don't be sorry. It's

been a long time and I am at peace with it now."

"We should get to know each other. Tell me the little things, funny things, things that make you you. What's your favorite color? Do you like to swim? Stuff like that."

Hearing his chuckle in my head made my toes curl up in my slippers. Something about him made me feel so comfortable. I wasn't even embarrassed that my string of questions sounded like those a kindergartner might ask when meeting a new person.

Before he could answer any of the questions I blurted out, "Can you turn into a human? I'm sorry if that's too nosy."

He huffed, and I could feel his frustration. "As alpha, the curse that has taken my pack's ability to shift does not affect me in quite the same way. I often feel like the change is imminent, that if I just push a little harder, I could do it. But so far I can't. The rest of the pack tells me that they do not feel their ability to shift at all, as if it is completely blocked from them."

His admission sends me into deep thought. Breaking the curse must be possible, after all, none of them are forever, were they? And it seemed like he would be the likely candidate for a first attempt, if I could locate the instructions. Perhaps the needed spell could be found somewhere within the books in the attic.

"Leah? You're just standing there, nose all scrunched up and tapping your finger to your lips. What are you thinking about?"

"Ha, sorry. I tend to do that when I'm focusing on a problem. I was just thinking, there has to be a way to break the curse, and you seem to be the best one to attempt it with. If I can restore your abilities, then the rest of the pack should be able to do so also. Right?"

"It sure would be amazing if you could. We'd all be grateful. And green. My favorite color is green. Yes, I like to swim, just not in the stream. It's the source of the curse, we think. Sometimes I travel out to the ocean and play in the waves. It's not too far from where the pack lives."

His ability to weave the answers to my inane questions with the very important subject of breaking the curse makes me giggle. An image formed in my mind of this huge gray wolf, frolicking in and out of the waves on the beach.

"I love the beach."

"I'd love to take you one day, if we get the chance."

Our eyes met and something passed between us

that I didn't understand. Considering that we'd barely just met, it seemed like we had known each other forever. Perhaps it was the situation we found ourselves in, thrown together by forces outside of our control. My imagination couldn't help but be curious about what he looked like in his human form...

"Earth to Leah! I lost you there again."

This time I blushed, knowing where my thoughts had been headed. "Sorry."

"I have to get back to the pack. It was nice meeting you though. Read your aunt's books, they should be able to teach you much of the magic you need to learn at this stage. I'm no witch, but I'll try to answer your questions if I can."

"I'll do the best I can. But, like I said, I just discovered this whole world of magic existed. I am a brand new witch and so far not a very impressive one. My most intricate spell can create light, and I can set things on fire. There are a few others that might come in handy someday, but many of the easy ones don't seem like they'd be super helpful in besting an evil spirit, unless she wants to roast marshmallows or something."

His laughter echoed through my head. "You'll do great, I promise. You were born for this, and the sanctuary has chosen you as its ally. The Mark will help you to grow and control your powers. You just have to have faith in yourself. Start small and don't overdo it. You can work your way up to the bigger spells as you learn. Come on, I'll walk you back to the clearing."

A nod and a smile were all I could muster up at the thought of his whole pack relying on me. We walked side by side for the few yards until we could see the back porch.

"Will I see you again soon?"

His head bobbed up and down. "Yes. I think we'll be seeing a lot of each other. I promise to do what I can to help you help us. But you'd better get inside now. I'll stay here till you get in the door."

Goodbyes said, I crossed the clearing and put my hand on the knob, pausing with the door open only a couple of inches. Wanting to catch one last look at him, I turned back around. His thundercloud gray coat disappeared just feet past the treeline. As soon as the moonlight became blocked by the branches, he disappeared without a trace.

Slipping inside and checking to be sure the handle was locked, I slumped against the door. My brain was becoming overloaded from all the new things it was trying to take in.

"Where have you been?"

My mother's stern tone startled me and I jumped, ramming my sore elbow into the doorjamb. Pain shot up my arm. I flipped the light switch to see her leaning against the counter with a mug in her hands.

"Ouch. Shit! What are you doing down here? Why aren't you asleep? You scared the crap out of me. Why are you just standing here in the dark, instead of turning a light on?"

"I could be asking the same of you. I couldn't sleep, so I came down to make some tea. I did my best to be quiet, so as not to wake you up, but imagine my surprise when I saw you come slinking out of the woods and trying to sneak back in the house. In the middle of the night, no less. How long were you out there and what were you doing?"

"Stop it. I'm a grown woman. And I wasn't *slinking* across the clearing, I walked. Which is the common method of transportation for humans traveling under their own power? Nor did I *sneak* back into the house. I was attempting to be quiet and considerate, so I didn't wake you up and disturb your rest. I know you need your sleep, especially with all of this added stress."

"And you don't think it might add to my stress to know you are out running around in the woods where your aunt died less than forty-eight hours ago?"

"Mom, I'm sorry. For one, I had no idea you were going to wake up or I would have left you a note so you didn't worry. It wasn't a planned outing, anyway. Kind of a spur-of-the-moment thing."

"The only thing that will keep me from worrying will be you promising me that you'll stay inside after dark. The animals that live on this land are not house pets, Leah. They will injure you, perhaps worse. Look what happened to Aimee."

"Mom, Aunt Aimee was not killed by any animal within this sanctuary, and we both know it." I kept my tone soft, knowing she needed me to be the rational one at the moment. The effects of the stress were beginning to show.

"I just can't bear the thought of losing you too." She choked back a sob.

Leaving my post by the back door, I walked across the kitchen to where she stood. Taking the mug from her hands, I set it on the counter behind her and gave her a hug. She never returned the gesture, although I felt her body relax beneath my arms. Guilt for making her worry wormed its way into the pleasure I'd felt from the late night walk and meeting Isaiah.

"Mom, I really am sorry. Let's go back to bed. I promise to not to go back out, I need my sleep too. Tomorrow we can talk some more, okay?"

"Something about this place is getting to you, with all this talk of magic and spells. The next thing you know you'll be telling me there are werewolves and vampires that live in the woods."

CHAPTER SIX

Strange dreams interrupted my sleep throughout the night, interrupting my chance at getting any real rest. Malevolent mist snaked through the trees of the sanctuary, beckoning me. The waters of the stream churned and swirled, trying to entice me into entering the water. Pages ripped from the books in the attic burned to ash before my eyes, the acrid smell causing me to gag and choke. Tears filled my eyes at the thought of all that information going up in smoke.

Jerking awake, I shuddered at the sweat dripping

down my sides, adhering the nightshirt to my skin like Plaster of Paris. Shards of the dream flitted through my memories, making it difficult to grasp any single message. The wind crept through the crack that the window had been left open. A wolf howled, the mournful sound filling the room. A glance at the clock told me I'd been dreaming for at least six hours and might as well get up. There would be no going back to sleep this morning.

Grabbing the most useful of my aunt's books to practice with, I headed down towards the kitchen, surprised to smell coffee already percolating.

"What are you doing awake already? It's awfully early."

My mom sat at the table, hands wrapped around a mug, staring off into space. The dim morning light bathed her in a grayish tint, making her look older than her years. At first she gave no acknowledgment that she even heard me, but then slowly turned to look at me. The purplish bags under her eyes made me feel guilty, wondering if she had been up all night because of me. Or whether the dreams that had haunted me all night affected her as well.

"I couldn't sleep." She sighed. "I haven't slept that

well at all since I got the call. I don't know if it's the loss, or sleeping here when I know she's gone, or what the hell is going on."

Oof. My mother never cussed. Ever. Pausing in the middle of pouring coffee, my gaze slid back to her, taking in the details. Tiny lines radiated from the corners of her eyes. At fifty-one, strands of silver had begun infiltrating her head of dark hair. Over the last couple of days her skin seemed to thin over her bones, causing her features to stand out more sharply against her face.

Before Aunt Aimee's death, my own mother's mortality had been a whisper in the back of my mind. One is always cognizant of the fact that nobody lives forever, however, until you lose someone close to you, the impact of such knowledge remains blissfully distant. The desire to comfort her, as a way to stave off the inevitable, rushed through me.

"I'm sorry, Mom. I should be more attentive to your feelings. Is there anything I can do to help out? I bet I could find a spell that would help you to get some sleep, at least."

"No! No spells. The last thing I need is you using me as a guinea pig to practice your so-called magic on." She jerked at the suggestion, sloshing her coffee over the side of the mug and onto the tabletop.

Her vehemence shocked me, the venom in her tone causing me to step back against the counter, bumping my hip against the edge. For a second I just stared, hurt that she would accuse me of using her as a guinea pig for anything. Pushing my shock aside, I turned away to grab a paper towel, using the moment to blink back the tears that welled up.

"I'm sorry, I..." I tried to apologize as I attempted to clean up the mess.

She put her hand over mine, taking the napkin from me, cutting me off mid-sentence. "No, I'm sorry. That was uncalled for, and I didn't mean it. I know you would never use me as a guinea pig. I just don't buy into the whole magic thing."

"Mom, then how do you explain the things I have learned to do since coming here? Answer me that."

"I may not be able to explain everything, but for now I would appreciate if you left me out of it. Turning little lights on and off is far different from trying to cast a spell on an actual human being. What if you made a mistake or messed up the spell? The consequences could be disastrous for me, and you might not be able to reverse them with your limited experience."

"Mom," before I could finish the sentence, she stood up.

"I think the lack of sleep is getting to me. That must be it. I'm not usually this clumsy. We both know you didn't get it from me." She tried to smile at our inside joke about my lack of grace. "I'm going to go try to take a nap."

"Okay," I called to her retreating backside as she walked down the hall.

Filling my mug the rest of the way and adding copious amounts of cream and sugar, my attention turned to the book of spells. Perhaps one existed that would create a sense of calm and peace in her room, allowing her to sleep better without me using magic on her directly. The thought of using magic to influence her when she had specifically asked me not to made me feel bad, but I wanted to help her somehow.

Isaiah had warned me to take things slow while learning, but my inexperience prevented me from knowing which spells would be considered easier and less taxing without actually trying them. Some of the ones I tried the first day took more effort than the words on the page appeared to require. Trial and error showed me what reading the words could not. I had no other way of gauging the difficulty. Too bad they didn't come with a rating system of some sort.

Three hours of practicing at the kitchen table left me with a need for some Tylenol and a weariness I could feel in my bones. The coffee had long since gone cold, and my stomach demanded some sort of sacrifice to appease the grumbling gods of my appetite. A quick look showed the pantry door cracked open, begging me to raid it for sustenance. In my distraction, I knocked a stack of cans, chicken noodle soup, from their perch, sending them rolling across the shelf and onto the floor. Muttering about my clumsiness, I returned them to their place and continued on my hunt for something appealing to eat.

As I rooted around in the cupboards for anything good to snack on, a sudden chill went down my back, alerting me that I was no longer alone.

"Mom? Is that you?"

No answer. Peering down the hall, I was able to see that her bedroom door hadn't opened since she went in to take her nap. The chill came again, this time pulling my interest toward the woods out back. From the shadows, a pair of amber eyes stared at the house.

Isaiah. He'd come to see me again.

Opening the back door to show him I'd be out in a minute, I left a hastily scribbled note on the table so my mom would know I'd gone for a walk and not been kidnapped right out from under her nose. I smoothed my hair as best I could without being able to see myself. Grabbing the book and a jacket, I slipped out the back door. In my haste I missed the second step, sending me staggering and dropping the book into the dirt. Grimacing, I picked it up and crossed the clearing into the trees, pretending I hadn't just embarrassed the shit out of myself in front of him.

My ankle ached, causing me to limp a little as I walked, but I tried to ignore it. He remained a gentleman and did not mention my humiliating stumble, even to ask if I was hurt.

"Hey you."

Despite the fact that we could talk telepathically, the act of speaking out loud made our conversation feel more normal to me. For some reason magic felt more understandable to me than communicating without using a voice. Which made me curious about something.

"Why couldn't I hear your voice in the house? Is there a distance limit of some sort? Did you ask me to come outside?" Questions poured from my lips, not giving him time to answer any of them.

He shook his head. "It was kind of an experiment. I wanted to see if you could feel me out here first. If you hadn't responded, then I planned to use our communication. How did you know I was out here?"

"Well, at first I just got the sensation that I wasn't alone anymore. Once I confirmed that my mom was still napping, I went back to the kitchen and felt the same sort of chill. When I looked out the window, I could see your eyes and just knew it was you."

"I guess next time I'll keep my eyes closed then." His chuckle rumbled through me.

"Nope. Don't do that. If it hadn't been for seeing them, I wouldn't have come outside at all. There is no way I'll be checking out strange sensations alone. Not now that I know funny things are happening here in the sanctuary."

"That's smart. But I think as we get to know each other better, you will be able to tell when it is me. You'll learn to recognize my presence just like if you saw me in person and recognized me."

"Well. If I saw you in person right now, I wouldn't recognize you! I've only seen you like this." My hand waved vaguely in his direction. "Except for your eyes. If they don't change, I bet I would know those eyes anywhere."

Heat crept up my cheeks at the insinuation that I knew him intimately enough to recognize him only by his eyes. This was only our second real meeting. The wind gusted through the trees, causing me to shiver.

"Do you need to go back inside?" I could feel his concern for me.

"Not yet. I've been practicing with my aunt's books, but it upsets my mom. We had a bit of an argument before she headed off to take a nap. She doesn't want anything to do with magic."

"That's odd. You'd think since she is Aimee's sister they would both be witches, wouldn't you?"

"I don't know how those things are passed through families, but I can guarantee you my mother doesn't have a magical bone in her body. Perhaps Aunt Aimee got all the magic, since she was the older sister, and my mom just got none."

"I don't know much about it either, but I suppose that is possible." He looked up at me. "I think we need to make a trip to the temple soon so we can see if we can learn any more about how your aunt actually died. I think that's the best place to start looking for clues, don't you?"

The thought of seeing where Aimee's body had lain gave me the creeps, but only because I knew that she hadn't just fallen dead of a heart attack. Someone or something had murdered her, right where she lay when we saw her last. And it made me so very mad. How dare they kill her? And why? She was the nicest person I'd ever met in my entire life.

"I think it's time," I answered him slowly. "I know I'm not going to get the answers to those questions by reading her books. I've looked through the house, and read some of the journals, but haven't got much information that might help figure it out. Clues, yes, but not answers."

"I'll go with you, of course. You won't have to go alone."

"Thank you. I don't know if I could bring myself to go in again if I needed to do it by myself. There is something dark and scary about that place, despite the fact that it is beautiful to look at and I would love to learn more about it someday."

"How is tomorrow for you? Are you busy?"

Before I could answer, the feeling that we were

being watched crept over me again. The little piece of sky I could see through the treetops became tinged with a blue that wasn't normal. Switching to speaking in his head let him know what I felt, and he agreed, hurrying me toward the clearing and the safety of the house.

"Go. Get inside. Aimee's house is the safest place in the sanctuary. I'll see you tomorrow."

"What about you?"

"I'll be fine, get inside. Hurry."

There was a push in his voice on the last word, conveying his urgency so I didn't argue. I ignored the pain in my ankle and rushed across the ground, watching my footing as I climbed the two stairs to the porch. Slipping in the back door, I turned to watch out the window, but he had already disappeared from sight.

My eyes strained to see through the shadows that danced between the trees, looking for anything that seemed out of place or threatening. The blue tint had faded, and I couldn't pin down anything else visually, but my gut told me that something was out there, just outside of my range of sight. Whatever it was, it didn't seem to want to make friends.

"Leah? What are you doing?"

I jumped at my mother's voice. "Looking outside.

Did you have a nice nap?"

"Well, I got some sleep at least. Hopefully not so much that I won't be able to sleep again when it's time for bed. What have you been doing?"

"I'd like to learn more about the ruins and the temple. Do you know where would be the best place to look for information?"

"Jesus, Leah. Why can't you just leave well enough alone? There is no reason to go poking your nose about in the ruins. They're dangerous and you could get hurt."

"Your sister *died* there. Of course there is a reason. Why don't you want to know what really happened to her?"

"She had a heart attack. That's all. No amount of poking around and playing with magic will bring her back. Just let it go, Leah. Stop all this nonsense."

"I think you know way more about all this than you want to tell me."

"Leah, we are done having this discussion. You are not to enter the ruins under any circumstances. I forbid it."

Grinding my teeth to keep from snapping at her, I counted to fifteen before finally speaking. "I am a grown adult, must I remind you of this again? And, as you so kindly pointed out to me, this property is mine now. Aunt Aimee left it to me, and I have every right to learn about it and explore it as I see fit. I'm sorry that upsets you, I really am, but that isn't going to stop me from doing it. If you won't help me, then I will figure it out on my own."

"Why must you be so unreasonable? It's as if your aunt's death made you pig-headed and stubborn, the way you all of a sudden refuse to listen to reason."

"Listen to reason? You mean because I have the audacity to remind you that I am a grown adult, not a toddler, and you are no longer in a position to be telling me what I can and can't do."

Her brows drew together, and she blew the air out through pursed lips. "Fine. You're right, I can't stop you. But I will tell you this. All of this futzing around with magic will find you way in over your head. If you don't back off, you are going to get yourself killed, just like Aimee."

CHAPTER SEVEN

Isaiah arrived as I sat rocking on the porch swing with my unicorn mug full of coffee the next morning. Things between my mother and I had been strained since the afternoon before, and smoothing them over didn't interest me in the least. Her attitude toward magic grated on my nerves and made me wonder just what she was hiding. Nobody who knew absolutely nothing about magic would realistically be so against the very idea of it.

"Ready?" He remained just out of sight, behind the

tree line and shrouded in the shadows.

Joining him, a slight pang of guilt twinged for not telling my mother where I'd be, but it disappeared at the sight of the wolf with amber eyes. The desire to run my hands through his fur was so intense it made my fingers ache, but I managed to refrain from reaching out.

"Let's go. I practiced a few spells that I thought might be helpful while we are there. One for becoming aware of things that might otherwise go unnoticed, and one for protecting us from the influence of spirits with negative intentions. There are a few others, but those seemed like they'd be the most helpful."

"Sounds good. If things get out of hand, I will get you out of there no matter what, I promise. I'm not going to let the same thing happen to you that happened to your aunt." His eyes met mine in earnest as he reassured me.

The reminder that I would be standing in the same building where Aunt Aimee had been murdered gave me goosebumps. Then the thought that he cared for my well-being and safety gave me shivers of a whole other kind.

"We'll get out of there together. But I don't see this as being a big deal yet. We're just going to look around, and hopefully won't draw any attention to ourselves."

"Our presence there may be enough to upset the spirit, but we'll see."

We walked side by side, not speaking, both of us immersed in our own thoughts. As we drew closer to the ruins, the air became oppressive, making it hard to breathe. Isaiah raised his nose, attempting to read the scents on the air. Both of us stopped at the crumbling wall that marked the edge of the ruins.

"I can feel the darkness. It just flows outward in waves from the building." My skin crawled at the feeling of it washing over me.

"The spirit must be contained here then. All the clues we have so far point to this being the place. We were right. Can you tell anything else without going inside?"

My eyes drifted closed as I tried to process the overwhelming sensations. Being so new at magic left me at a severe disadvantage when it came to interpreting the messages I picked up. My conscious mind strained, attempting to grasp things that floated just out of my realm of understanding. Pressure against my leg caused me to open my eyes and look down. Isaiah had leaned against me.

Physical contact with him seemed to increase my focus. Closing my eyes again, I reached down and slid my fingers through the fur on his back. Feeling the smirk on my lips, I hoped he had his eyes trained on the ruins and not my face.

Awareness of the spirit became pinpointed on an underground room, accessed from somewhere in the temple itself. The spell held, but minuscule cracks radiated through it. As the spirit grew in power, the spell would continue to fail. We needed to do something before it became too late.

Using the telepathic communication we shared, I let Isaiah see everything I could. I wanted him to know what we were dealing with as clearly as possible. He tensed beneath my hand, reminding me that I still had hold of his fur.

"Sorry."

He exhaled. "It's not you. This just seems to be corroboration that all the legends and stories are true. The wolves within the sanctuary have lost many of their memories, and the ones they do retain are muddled and inaccurate. We couldn't be sure if it was due to being stuck in our wolf forms for so long, or something else. Now I think it may be both."

"There must be a way to fix it. As alpha I would think it would be easiest to cure you first, since you're among the strongest of the wolves, if you don't mind being a guinea pig for a spell or two?"

"From regal wolf to wheeking guinea pig, sounds splendid." He snorted.

"I promise not to actually turn you into a guinea pig!" I paused. "Probably."

"Oozing with confidence, that's the way to round up volunteers."

Before I could come up with a witty retort, a wave of unease flooded me. Returning my attention to the stones in front of us, I waited to see if something else came through. Turning to Isaiah, I started to speak but was interrupted.

"Whoa!"

"What is it?"

"Your eyes are turning blue. I think we need to get out of here. Let's go. We can talk more when we are a safe distance away from this place."

As we turned and went back the way we had come, I felt the sensations of being watched, certain that if I turned around to look there would be a million pairs of eyes watching us go. Isaiah led the way to a clearing in the trees, set up as sort of a meeting place. Logs had been laid horizontally for seating, branches and bark stripped from them. A ring of stones created a fire pit directly in the middle.

"Where are we?" I sat on a log and he plopped down in front of me.

"This is a meeting place we sometimes used, before all of us became stuck in wolf form. It's safe here, and we aren't all that far from your house."

"Getting back to the guinea pig situation..." I waited for him to protest, and when he didn't I continued. "I spent a lot of time working on a spell that will allow me to look inside and maybe see the curse. I promise not to try and do anything, I just want to know if it would be possible for me to learn how it works so I can eventually remove it. My hope is that I would also be able to unlock your ability to shift again."

"You want to look inside my mind?"

"Sort of. I promise I'm not looking for your deepest, darkest secrets or anything. Although I have never done this before, so I can't guarantee that I won't see something I'm not actually looking for. This spell is a counter-spell of sorts, to be able to understand a spell that has been cast on someone. Wow, how many times can I say the word spell in a sentence?"

"Spell, spell, spell, spell..." he laughed. "Wheek, wheek," he imitated a guinea pig quite well. "All kidding aside, I trust you. I think it's worth the risk, Besides, there isn't much exciting to see in there, anyway."

"Wow. To be honest, I kind of expected you to say no. Like, a resounding hell no!" In spite of the fact that it had been my idea, I hesitated to actually attempt to dig around in someone else's brain.

"Nah. Like I said, I don't have anything to hide. And if I can get my ability to shift back, that means we can eventually help the rest of my pack, and that is a sacrifice I, as alpha, need to be willing to make."

Sliding off the log, I sat cross-legged in the dirt directly in front of him. "The book says powerful witches can do the spell without any physical contact, but just to be sure I'd like to lay my hands on you so we are connected. Is that alright?"

"Well, I thought you'd never ask."

My face turned tomato red at his teasing. Could he feel how much I wanted to touch him, or was he just a flirt?

"I'm just kidding; you don't have to be embarrassed. Sorry to tease you, I just couldn't help it.

Go ahead and do what you need to do, and I promise to behave. I won't even lick your face."

"Ha." Even that single syllable choked me as I imagined him licking me. "Okay, I am going to put my hands on either side of your shoulders, and I want our foreheads to touch. That will give me the best opportunity to connect with you. I think. This will have to be a little bit trial and error."

He bent forward until our foreheads touched. "Like this?"

Even in wolf form, there was something so deeply human about his eyes that I found myself lost in them. My hands found their way to his shoulders with no instructions from my brain needed. I threaded my fingers through his fur, tugging on him slightly to pull him just a little bit closer. The desire to return his ability to shift stemmed from an entirely selfish place.

"Leah?"

Startled, I yanked my hands back, pulling on his fur in the process, while scrambling to gain control of my wayward daydreams. "Sorry, I was just trying to be sure I was ready. And I am kind of surprised you don't have doggy breath."

Mortified at what had just come out of my lips, I

slapped my hand over my mouth. If anyone had ever been unsure about whether canines could look incredulous, they can. Oh, so well. Their eyebrows can raise just as obviously as those on any human face. My embarrassment at being caught having less than pure thoughts about a wolf immediately replaced itself with the humiliation of having been outright rude.

He sat silently watching me for a minute before bursting out laughing. His mirth echoed through my head. His hilarity at the situation drove him to act like an actual wolf, flopping onto his side and making chuffling sounds that could only be described as doggy laughter.

"Are you quite finished?" I harrumphed at him in the haughtiest tone I could manage.

"You should have seen your face!" he hooted with laughter as he forced the words.

"That's it. I'm going to turn you into a guinea pig for real now."

"Oh no, anything but that..." He returned to sit in front of me, taking up the same position as before.

Taking a handful of fur, I gave it a little yank. "Hey. Pay attention." I winked at him. "Let's get on with this, shall we?"

I could still feel him shaking with laughter as he tried to hold it back. My head tilted forward, and I kept a stranglehold on my imagination as I touched my forehead to his. The words to the practiced spell fell from my lips naturally as I reached out to find the information I sought. The first attempt netted me nothing but blackness.

"Nothing. I'll need to try again, but I think I need a second."

"No rush. And it doesn't have to happen today, remember that. No pressure."

"That's nice of you to say, but in reality I don't think time is on our side. That evil spirit, whatever it is. will only continue to grow stronger. I need to get it right. Let's try again."

So we tried again. And again. And then again. By the fourth attempt I had managed to carve out a path that led me to what I needed to see, the next step would be to understand it.

"What about the spell you practiced to use at the temple if we needed it, to see things you might not otherwise see? Can you combine the two of them?"

"Well, I can definitely try. That's an excellent idea. Let's see where it gets us."

Ignoring the headache forming in my frontal lobe, I leaned forward once more. As our foreheads met once more, I barely needed to expend any effort to get to the place where the spell had sunk itself into his psyche. Once there, I switched the words, and began chanting the ones that he had suggested. Over and over I repeated them, watching in awe as the tangle of information slowly made itself clear to me.

Bits and pieces floated about, many of them making perfect sense. But dark holes also filled the space, places that no matter how hard I focused, I could not break through their secrets. My eyes opened as I sighed in frustration to find him staring back at me.

"Leah. Your nose is bleeding. Are you hurt? Was it some sort of spell to harm you?"

"No," I responded. "I think I just went too far. Operating above my pay grade, ya know? My brain and body decided they've had enough." I wiped the offending blood on the sleeve of my sweatshirt. "I'll be fine."

"What did you see? Did you learn how to help me? Us?"

"I managed to get some of it. But I think to truly understand the curse I need to go to a stream. I kept getting glimpses of running water, and riverbanks. The curse is somehow tied to a stream. I've got a good base of information though, and once I can find the stream, I think it will give me the rest of the pieces to the puzzle."

"There is only one stream that runs through the sanctuary. It begins on the far eastern side, where there is a small mountain range, really just one mountain and a couple of smaller peaks. There is a waterfall, and it is the birthplace of the stream. The stream then runs across almost the entire length of the peninsula and empties into the ocean at the northwest corner."

"Well, I guess that narrows our options then. I need to see it. Can you show me where it is?"

Isaiah started to shake his head, and his shoulders dropped. Then he straightened up. "All of the packs tend to avoid it, but I can take you if you think there isn't any other way."

His hesitation swamped me. "You can just tell me where it is, if you want. You don't have to go. But why do the wolves avoid it?"

Eyes closed, he sat quietly for a few seconds. "I can't remember," he answered when he opened his eyes again. "I don't know why, that is just how it has been for a long time."

"Okay, well, I can find it if you tell me where to go. I doubt I will have to go all the way to the waterfall, since I didn't see one in any of the visions I got of the curse."

"I can't let you go alone. Follow me. It's not a terribly far walk from here, and we have plenty of daylight left."

CHAPTER EIGHT

"The straightest line there has no cleared pathway, but it shouldn't be too hard if you follow me. That is, if you can trust a guinea pig not to get you lost in the forest." The irony in his tone made me smirk.

Before I could catch myself, I swatted him lightly on the rump. And a very muscular rump it happened to be. "Very funny." Oh my gosh, I was admiring the physical characteristics of a *dog*. What the hell was wrong with me?

He yelped and pretended to run away. "OW!" He

circled me as we walked, whining and pretending to be injured.

"I'm telling you, I will learn a spell to turn you into a toad if you leave me stranded in these woods all alone!" His antics made me laugh and I couldn't help but think what fun he might be in human form.

Sounds of the water rushing in the stream bed reached my ears long before I could see it. The gurgling sounds told me that this area was not a calm babbling brook, but more of a rushing river in spite of its moniker of "stream," at least at this section. Isaiah's footsteps slowed. The closer we crept, the slower his feet moved. An oppressive feeling hung in the air. Every breath I took felt like I was trying to suck in oil instead of oxygen.

The blue waters rushed over smooth river pebbles, the water so clear I could see right to the bottom. Sand flanked the banks, running right up until it met the trees. While the occasional leaf floated along on the current, there was no other detritus to be seen within its water. No sticks or water plants, not even a fish. In spite of the outward beauty, something ominous clung to the waterway.

"What's wrong with this place?" I asked him in a

whisper, as if something in the forest might have ears and be listening to my words.

"This is how the stream has felt for years. Any time we get near it. It used to beckon us, trying to entice us to drink of its waters. After a while it began driving us away. At one time, when I was pretty small, it used to be the place we came to have picnics and play in the water. I can't remember exactly when that changed, but it changed overnight, and has been this way for years."

"I'm going to check it out. You should wait here, just in case."

He followed me to the edge of the water anyway, as I knew that he would. The water itself looked innocent enough. As I knelt down to touch it, I felt his teeth clamp on to my sleeve as he pulled me backwards.

"Don't touch it. It might only be harmful to wolves, but what if it does something bad to you too? We need you to be whole."

"I don't think it would hurt me. I'm not a shifter, so it can't block my ability to change. But I will wait until I get more information, just to be sure. Better safe than sorry."

He paced along the bank, peering into the woods on the other side occasionally, while I tried to find clues as to what might be happening with the stream. Deciding that I'd seen all that was possible with the naked eye, I prepared to do the spell I'd practiced for use at the temple.

"I want to try the spell for things I wouldn't notice otherwise. I'm going to sit here and close my eyes. Can you keep watch for me, please? Just in case, the last thing I want is to be caught off-guard if trouble shows up."

"Of course, you don't even need to ask. I've got your back. And your front, too."

Settling myself in the dry sand, a few feet back from the water's edge, I began focusing on the words of the spell and the information I needed. My witchy sight, as I had begun calling it, played images against the backs of my eyelids, almost like a movie playing in real time. The problem was, it was like a poorly recorded mish mash of events.

A figure stood at the water's edge, chanting. Their form distorted by the cloak they wore, with its hood up over their head, hid even the sex of the person, preventing me from knowing if I was looking at a male or female. Only the small stature led me to think female. The blurring of the image made it impossible to recognize, but their actions were obvious. Removing a small vial or bottle from either their pocket or a bag at their side, they removed the lid and poured a substance into the river. The chanting continued until the entire contents had been emptied into the water.

Once the liquid washed downstream, the waters changed. They morphed from what you would expect a stream running through a forest to look like, filled with sticks, leaves and animals, to the crystal clear waters I saw before me. Vapors shaped loosely like the humanoid figure rose from the surface and then sank back under, taunting any who came near.

As I sat trying to unravel the curse, I paid no mind to the misty figures, until it was too late. One of them had wandered close enough to make contact with me, latching on. It broadcast its intention loud and clear. To steal my energy and drag me to the stream, carrying me away. Struggling to open my eyes, I couldn't break the hold it had on me. My body felt leaden and unable to function. My brain grappled to make sense of what was happening.

Fear poured through my veins. Why didn't Isaiah do something? Could he not see I struggled right before his eyes? Desperate, I reached out to speak to his mind, instead of trying to use my voice.

I felt his surprise as I screamed for help. Blackness edged my vision. I couldn't make my muscles obey the commands to fight, to get up and run, to do *something.* The last thing I remembered was hearing Isaiah's voice telling me to hold on. But I couldn't hold on anymore.

A sharp pain in my forehead pulled me from unconsciousness. Blinking away the double vision, I rubbed my face, confused about where I was and why I lay on the forest floor. Angry chattering filled the air above me, interspersed with deep growls. Rubbing my forehead, I tried to focus on my new surroundings.

"Uh, what the hell is happening here?"

Isaiah returned to my side immediately. "Oh, thank goodness you're conscious. I didn't think you were ever going to wake up."

"Where are we?" Up in the tree sat a pair of chipmunks, chattering loudly. One held a pine cone in its tiny paws. "Were those critters throwing pine cones at me?"

"I'm sorry, I tried to stop them, but they are way out of reach." He turned toward them and growled once more.

"It's okay, I think that's what finally brought me

around. And I am almost certain they are the same ones I saw the first day we arrived, and then again in my aunt's attic somehow."

Pulling myself into a sitting position, I winced as my lower back protested at the movement. My head ached and my vision still hadn't returned to normal. I relayed everything I could remember to Isaiah at his request, trying not to leave out any of the sketchy details. When I finished, he paused before responding.

"It was the strangest thing. You were sitting there all peaceful and calm. It was taking a while, but since you didn't seem distressed, I just waited. Then all of a sudden I could hear you screaming in my head. I couldn't see or feel anything, but assumed the stream must be the source of the problem, so I drug you as far from it as I could. You're probably going to feel some bumps and bruises, so I'm sorry. In this form I can't carry you very gently."

I looked up at him, since he towered over me when we were both in a sitting position, and sighed. "Don't be sorry, I appreciate the rescue. It's a crazy hard spell to understand, especially for someone like me, who has limited experience. I need to go back and read through my aunt's books. She had to have known that something was wrong with the stream and made notes about it somewhere. I at least have a good idea of what I'm looking for now."

The web of magic was complex and difficult to unravel. More research would be needed before I could even attempt to break the curse.

"It's getting dark; we need to hurry back. You were out for quite a while before the little pine cone pitchers came along. I couldn't leave you alone on the ground, but I was beginning to worry we were going to need help. I'm okay out here at night, but I don't want you to be out so deep in the woods. Aimee's house is safe. Out here could be dangerous. Some of the wolves have been trapped in their animal forms for a long time and aren't always easy to reason with."

He let me lean against him to get off the ground, and I grimaced at the sharp pain that shot through my hip. The walk back would seem ten times longer than it really was, of that I had no doubt. The pair of chipmunks ran from tree to tree, shadowing us the entire way. I owed them a reward of some kind for saving my bacon, even if their methods left a little to be desired.

Isaiah stopped short of the clearing, saying he'd be sure I got to the door before taking off. My little rodent friend's ran ahead of me, taking cover under the back deck. With one last look his way, and a smile, I left Isaiah in the forest to return to the house.

My aunt's pantry had no nuts that I could find, but Ritz crackers seemed like a reasonable treat for my saviors and I carried a small handful outside.

"Hey guys? If you're out here, I brought you a snack. A little thank you for helping me out back there. I really appreciate it."

They didn't appear, so I set the crackers on the side table next to the porch swing and went back inside. Hopefully they would discover the treats even if they didn't understand or hear my words. My mother entered the kitchen from the hall.

"I thought I heard you come in. You look like you took a tumble down a very tall hill. Where have you been, and who were you talking to?"

I laughed a little at her second question, suddenly embarrassed to be caught talking to little forest creatures. Who did I think I was, Snow White?

"I was just out exploring in the woods. And I was talking to a pair of resident chipmunks I've seen hanging around. I know Aunt Aimee used to feed some of the animals who came close to the house, and I think they were looking for a snack." I refrained from telling her I thought there was more to the pair than one would think. "I set some crackers outside for them, since they didn't come when I offered them." I shrugged at my explanation.

She shook her head, telegraphing her amusement with my answer. "Feeding the squirrels, are you? Okay, then. What do you want to do for dinner?"

Not bothering to correct her on the species of rodent, I lifted my shoulders. "Something easy if you don't mind? I'll be happy to throw together some soup and sandwiches once I have a quick shower."

"I'll start the soup; you can make sandwiches when you get out. Deal?"

Thankful she hadn't asked me any more questions, I nodded my agreement and escaped to the bathroom down the hall. Stripping my filthy clothes off, I examined myself in the mirror. A bright red strawberry covered my right hip, the scrapes angry and welted from being drug across the forest floor. My right shoulder blade suffered a similar fate, greenish bruising spread across my skin there. I picked all the pine needles I could find from my hair before stepping into the shower to wash away the grime, and hopefully the terrifying feeling that had been left behind by whatever had attacked me at the stream.

Watching the last of the grime swirl down the drain made me grimace at the amount of dirt I'd been covered in. While I shampooed my hair, I found even more pine needles and twigs. Too bad I could wash away the scrapes and bruises.

Dinner, even as simple as it was, went a long way towards helping me feel normal again, although I was still exhausted. Performing any sort of magic, even the easy stuff, seemed to squeeze all the energy from my body. Add to that my terrifying experience at the stream earlier, and I had nothing left to give for the day. Bidding my mother goodnight, I retired to bed to read through the books I had brought down, looking for any clues as to the curse on the stream.

If there wasn't anything in these three, I would have to head back up to the attic in the morning to look for another volume that might have more information. In spite of the many books I had read through, there were still boxes of them that I hadn't even cracked open yet. They didn't seem to be stored in any sort of order, leaving me to guess which ones I should choose next.

It occurred to me at that moment that there might

be a spell to lead me to the books containing the information I hoped to find, and I should try it the next time I went up to get more books. The worst thing that could happen is that it would give me something irrelevant, which wouldn't leave me any worse off than if I didn't do the spell at all.

Numerous references to the stream, and the curse, were peppered throughout each of the books. The bits and pieces helped my understanding of the problem, but gave me no real solution. The only place where a counter spell was referenced faced a page that had been torn from the book. Had Aunt Aimee found the spell? If so, why would she tear it out of the book?

CHAPTER NINE

The hours of reading had not brought me to an answer for reversing the curse on the stream, but I now believed I knew how to remove enough of the curse from Isaiah to return his ability to shift. It would be a step in the right direction. Gathering the supplies listed in the grimoire and packing them into a backpack, I prepared to head into the woods and see if I could call Isaiah to me, the same way he was able to reach me.

Thankful that my aunt kept all of her spell casting supplies neat and orderly in her office so time wasn't wasted on searching for them, I added a couple sandwiches to the bag, as well as some bottled water. Pausing at the thought of how much effort the spell would take, whether or not it was successful, I added more food. A couple of apples, some cookies and a package of beef jerky gave me enough calories to at least make it home, I figured. With lunches packed, I was ready to get going.

Letting my mother know I'd be gone for a while, and ignoring her sour face at the news, I slipped out the backdoor. Perched on the table where I'd left the crackers sat my two little friends.

"Hey guys. Did you like the crackers?"

Both of them responded with chatter, one of them running in circles around the table top.

"Do you want some more?"

More chatter. More skittering about the table.

"Okay, be right back."

Taking a couple from each box I found to give them a variety, I returned to the porch. Laughing at myself for making conversation with the furry little creatures, I handed over the crackers and let them know I'd be gone for a while. At least they didn't seem to disapprove of my plans for the day.

Following the path into the woods, I reached out for Isaiah with my mind. I'd never tried to use our telepathy from a distance and didn't know what kind of range I had. It occurred to me then that I had also never been to the village where their houses were, which meant I couldn't just walk over and see if he happened to be home.

If he didn't hear me, or couldn't answer me, then I'd just be puttering around the yard until he showed up. Hopefully, he would have a reason to come by today. If not, I would just keep practicing until I saw him again.

After walking down the path for a few minutes, I could hear his voice, loud and clear.

"Hey. Are you okay, Leah?"

"Fine. But I have something exciting I want to try. Are you busy right now?"

"Not really, what's up? I can start heading your way."

"Good. I think today is the day. I believe I have a spell so that I can return your ability to shift back to human form." My excitement bled into my tone, even telepathically.

"I'm on my way. Don't wander too far by yourself."

He came loping up the path minutes later.

Somewhat unsuccessfully, I tried to hide how excited I was to see him. And how nervous I felt about the spell. It would be the most complicated one I had attempted to cast since learning about magic. Hopefully, I'd end up with a human at the end of it, and not a toad or a guinea pig.

Isaiah wanted to return to the clearing where we had sat before, and I agreed. Wherever he wanted me to perform the ritual was fine with me. Once we got there, I pulled out my aunt's book and the supplies. Each instruction was followed to the letter, and I kept up a running commentary, explaining what I had found out as I worked.

Once the circle was cast on the dirt, I continued adding the other items to the set up according to the instructions. In my mind, I equated witchcraft and spell casting to baking. Each ingredient needed to be added in the correct order in order for you to get the desired outcome.

Standing back to survey my setup, I reread the directions one last time. The words had been repeated over and over, relentlessly committing them to memory so that there would be no errors in the order or pronunciation. Directing Isaiah to his place in the center of the circle, I took a deep, cleansing breath.

"You sure you trust me to do this?"

"Wheek, wheek. What am I, if not your faithful and loyal guinea pig?" he teased me.

"Shut up. I swear to God I will turn you into a toad someday and put you in a glass tank on my desk."

"Ha. Let's see if we can get me back to human first, shall we?"

As our laughter subsided, I set the book down and prepared to try it for real. I'd done it a thousand times in my head. I'd read the pages over and over again. The words had been repeated so many times I could pronounce them in my sleep after an entire bottle of wine.

But I'd never had my subject in front of me. The man -wolf- who had become my friend. He trusted me enough to place his faith in me that I wouldn't screw this up, and that somehow made the situation worse rather than better.

Based on my understanding of the situation, I would need to cast the spell while working to pull his human side forward. The curse needed to be removed and I would likely need to force his shift back for the first time. After that the passage said he would be able to shift back and forth at will, as he had always been intended to do, if we were successful.

"Basically, it's a simple game of tug-o-war. The curse wants to keep your ability to shift in and I want to drag it out. You'll need to push from your end too, though. For some reason I have this picture in my head of trying to force an elephant to walk on a leash, but we'll give it a shot."

"Got it. Thankfully, I haven't forgotten how to shift, so I will try my damnedest to push through."

"Okay, and do not stop until I tell you to, or you are shifted. Do not worry about me, I can do this. I promise." I slipped off my shoes and socks, sinking my toes into the earth and attempting to connect with mother nature.

"As long as it doesn't cause you harm, I won't. And fair warning, you might want to wait for me to let you know it's safe to open your eyes."

"Excuse me?"

"So, when we shift, we usually retain whatever clothes we were wearing and they return with us. But, I've been in wolf form for so long, I don't want you to get an unwanted eyeful if I wind up buck ass naked."

Unwanted? He must be out of his damn mind. In

spite of having never seen his human form, I just knew it would be a glorious sight. Not that I would tell him that.

"Uh, sure. You got it. Maybe I can call up some pants for you if the need arises."

"Let's just see how it goes first. Ready?"

Nodding so he'd know I was ready, I closed my eyes. The first two times I chanted the words, they stayed in my head. The third time they were spoken in a whisper as I lifted my arms to the sky, asking for the blessings of the sanctuary. Each successive time I raised the volume until I was speaking in a slightly louder than normal voice.

The magic of the ancient spell swirled up around me. The sensation traveled from my bare toes, dug into the forest floor, to the tips of my fingers, enhancing my senses. The smell of the woods around me intensified. Despite the distance, I could hear the waves of the surrounding ocean crashing against the shore, and the thunder of the waterfall from the opposite side of the peninsula. Miniature insect footsteps echoed in my ears, and the hum of tiny wings thrummed in the distance.

With each repetition of the sacred words, I used my mind to pull Isaiah closer to me, calling out to his human form, casting away the curse. Sweat beaded and ran down my body as I struggled to free him. At one point, I heard him groan, telling me he was so close to success.

The pressure of the magic caused my ears to pop, muting the sounds I'd been hearing so acutely. My hair floated on the electrically charged air, tugging at my scalp. My temperature ratcheted up, bringing more sweat to my skin. And still the curse resisted my effort to dispel it. It fought tooth and nail to keep its claw sunk into his psyche.

My arms moved to reach toward him, curling my hands into fists and pantomiming the act of pulling his body toward me. My fingers couldn't have strained more if I hung from a cliff using only them to anchor me. My muscles ached with the strain. I felt blood run from my nose. Tears leaked from under my eyelids. Then, in a single second, it ended.

My strength gave way like a chain link snapping, landing me on my knees on the forest floor, eyes still closed. Exhaustion prevented me from opening them, although I had no desire to see my failure. I rested my weight on my hands, too wrung out to attempt to stand. I felt each object against my skin, from the pine needles and small rocks digging into my palms to the lumps of dirt around them. The crescent mark on my palm was strangely sensitive to the sensations of the earth.

"You can open your eyes, Leah."

My head jerked up. I had heard that voice with my *ears.*

"Isaiah?"

My eyelids lifted by the millimeter. Once fully open, they stared straight into the amber eyes I had grown so familiar with over the last few days. Eyes that were set in a human face. They were framed in thick, dark lashes, resting above cheekbones that looked like they had been carved out of stone. He squatted in front of me with his hands held out, offering his assistance.

"Are you ready to stand up?"

Blinking rapidly, I attempted to dislodge the sensation of being lost. He stood, taking my hands and drawing me to my feet. Slipping his arm around my waist, he helped me to the log and sat me down. Grabbing one of the napkins I had thrown in with the sandwiches, he dumped some of the water from the bottle onto it and wiped my nose.

He handed me the bottle. "Here, drink. And once you're ready, you need to eat. I'm glad you brought food.

That sort of thing takes a lot out of your body."

"Thanks." My voice was little more than a hoarse croak. My entire body felt like it had been run over by a semi-truck, then thrown in front of a train, and steam rolled for good measure. It didn't hurt exactly, but it ached everywhere.

My eyes roamed his body, clad in a plain black t-shirt and jeans. His feet were bare. The brown hair caught me by surprise, since his wolf was gray. Making my way up to his face once more, I blushed, having been caught staring.

"I'm sorry. This is quite a change, and you've known what I look like forever."

He chuckled. "Do I meet your standards? Or am I so ugly you are going to re-curse me yourself and make sure I never get to leave my wolf form again?"

Lacking the energy to even giggle, I sighed. "Well, I mean, your wolf is very pretty. But I guess I'll let you stay as you are. After all, I didn't do all that work for nothing. Besides, now you owe me. It'll be easier to get my payback this way. And if I was going to curse you to an animal form, I'd have to say I'm picking a toad. Promises are promises, after all."

"I owe you alright, and believe me, I intend to make

sure you are sufficiently rewarded."

His words brought heat to my cheeks. He took out a sandwich and tore off a chunk, placing it at my lips.

"Here, eat."

And he fed me the entire sandwich that way, stopping to give me drinks from the water bottle between bites. Never in my adult life had someone been so attentive to my needs. The action only made me like him more.

"You should eat too. I made a sandwich for each of us, and there's some other food in there too."

After trying to insist that I eat them both, he gave in when I insisted I couldn't eat another bite, and took one for himself. Stealing glances from the side, I watched him bite off pieces and chew, finding the motion of his jaw to be very appealing.

Thanks to the sustenance gained from the food, I started to feel a bit more like myself as time went on. An exhausted and wrung out version of myself, but myself nonetheless.

He turned to face me, meeting my eyes with a serious look on his face. "Leah, thank you. I can't thank you enough for this. It's been so long I almost feel like a stranger in my own body. But I would never have gotten it back without you."

"You're welcome. And it's the least I could do. I just pray that at some point I have the power and the know-how to do the same for the rest of the pack. I hate that right now you're the only one who is getting any relief."

"Trust me, once I show them that it's possible, they will be thankful you even tried. The majority of the pack are good people. I think you'll really like them."

"The majority, huh?"

"Well, we have some characters just like any other community, but nobody is bad. They all know that any sort of behavior that is detrimental to the pack could get them banished."

Keeping my thoughts to myself, I silently wondered if that meant that they were all actually good, or if it just meant that they spent a lot of energy trying to hide their true nature. Not wanting to offend him, I decided to change the subject.

"So, as I studied the books looking for this spell, I did learn quite a bit about the curse, and the cloudy memories. I think with enough time I can find a way to reverse it."

CHAPTER TEN

"Much of the information in my aunt's book is spread out through the volumes. She wasn't the only one to write in them, obviously. It looks like there have been other women in my family who were witches also, although I think some of the entries are from women not related to us. Her coven, maybe, if she had one."

"I didn't know your aunt well enough to be able to say, but that would be a likely scenario. I doubt Aimee would have allowed any unreliable information to be entered into the books, so most of what you found should be accurate. The only hang up would be if things have changed, which would make some of it out of date."

"According to the information I read, in order to reverse a curse, it helps to know the caster of the spell. It said that each person who performs magic leaves behind a signature, like a magical fingerprint. Once you know who cast the spell, or curse, then you can begin to unravel it. You must learn their encryption and then you can work backwards, untangling it and rendering it harmless."

"I suppose that makes sense."

"Aunt Aimee must have figured out how the curse on the stream was cast and tried to reverse it. I wonder if that is what she was doing when she died?" My voice caught on the words.

She had died trying to help the shifters on the reserve because she didn't call for someone to help her. Tears streamed down my face. If she had called me and said she needed my help, I would have come.

Isaiah put his arm around my shoulder, pulling me close. With my face buried in my hands, I leaned against him. At this point, the pain of her loss stabbed me so deep that I wouldn't have turned down comfort from anyone.

"I'm so sorry, Leah. I wish there was something I could have done. Or something I can do to help you feel better. I know it sucks to lose someone close to you."

He held me for a few long minutes, giving me a chance to cry it out and collect myself when I finished. Using my sweatshirt sleeve to wipe the tears, I looked up at him.

"I must look like a real disaster, huh? Did you ever figure that once you got your ability to shift back, the first thing you'd be doing is consoling a crazy sobbing girl?"

I felt his chuckle rumble through his broad chest. "I mean, I suppose there are worse ways to spend my time, right? And you look beautiful, as always."

His reward was a tiny smile. "But I feel like such a failure. There is so much guilt. If I hadn't let my mom talk me out of coming to visit, so much of this might never have happened. For one, I'm sure she would have begun teaching me about magic, eventually. And if she had done that, then I would have been prepared to help her with the curse. If I had been coming to visit her, she never would have taken on the task alone. Between the two of us, we would have been enough."

"She wouldn't want you to feel guilty, Leah. You may not know them, but I bet she had her reasons for doing things the way she did."

"You're probably right, and my head knows, but my heart doesn't care. I'd give anything to bring her back. *Anything at all.*"

"I wish I could help you bring her back. But we can't. Even a magical spell won't bring her back to us."

My gaze went to the ground. Maybe there was a way to bring her back hiding in one of those books somewhere. I might not be strong enough yet, but if I practiced, maybe I could bring her back to us somehow.

Isaiah reached out and gently took my chin in his hand. He tilted my face upward until I met his eyes. "You can't bring her back. And I bet she wouldn't want you to. The magic that is this sanctuary doesn't work that way."

Blinking to drive away the thoughts crowding into my head, driven there by the nearness of his lips, I nodded.

"I just feel so damn helpless. I'm too weak with my magic to fix this mess, and I can't even begin to guess what it will take to get me where I need to be."

"My dad told me a story once, when I was feeling

down about things. I don't remember what I was upset about exactly. But, it's one of the few things I remember clear as the day that he taught me. He told me a story which I won't bore you with the entire thing because you aren't seven, but the basic premise was this." He closed his eyes for a moment before looking back at me. "Being strong is not about being able to do something all by yourself, or being able to do everything you *think* you *should* be doing. Being strong means being smart. Strength means asking for help when you know you need it, even if you don't want to do it. Weakness lies not in being wrong, but refusing to admit when you are so that you can turn things around to make them right. It means you keep going, even though something is hard and you want to lay down and give up."

"Wow. That's pretty deep to be teaching a seven-year-old."

"Maybe, but I can tell you this, it has stuck with me my entire life. When I lost my ability to shift, I wanted to lay down and die. I love my wolf, but I always knew I was a human first. My entire identity was tied to my humanity. But because that story lived in my head, I never gave up. I kept looking for the way, because I knew someday it would come. And here you are. I am sitting next to you, as myself, because I waited. You are strong. I can see it in you. You will keep going, not just because that is what your aunt would have wanted, but because you know you can make a difference. You proved that here today."

"Wow. You sure are good for a girl's ego." I winked at him. "Thank you for the pep talk, and sharing that piece of yourself with me. I needed it."

"I could see that." With a wink back, he looked around the forest and stood. "If you feel up to walking now, I think we need to get you home. It's getting late, and dark."

He held out his hand and pulled me to my feet. My muscles ached in protest, but I could manage. He slipped his arm through mine to give me support, and I took full advantage of his closeness.

By the time we reached the trail that led to the house, I had exhausted all that was left of my energy. We stopped just out of sight of the clearing.

"I'm going to return to my wolf form. I want to keep this between the two of us for a few days until I decide how to break it to the pack, if that's okay with you?"

"Well, sure. It's not like I've ever seen any of the

other inhabitants of this sanctuary, except for a tiny pair of chipmunks, who you met, and I use that term loosely, yesterday. Oh, and I've seen a few birds fly over, but none have stopped to chat. If I told my mother what I've spent today doing, she would probably have me sent to the loony bin."

"Alright, smarty pants, I get it. Let me just change and I'll walk you the rest of the way back."

"That's okay, it's right around the bend. I may have to crawl that last ten feet, but I'll make it. You can watch me round the corner from here if it makes you feel any better."

He grinned. "You got it. You can still reach me telepathically if you need me. I don't have to be in wolf form for us to use that type of communication."

With an awkward little wave, I turned and walked away from him, fighting the urge to turn around and take one last look at him. It took the majority of my focus just to place one foot in front of the other without falling. My muscles ached right down to my bones. Never before had I felt so physically depleted.

Crossing the back porch, I noted that the chipmunks were nowhere to be seen, but the crackers had all disappeared. They needed names. Just calling them "the chipmunks" wasn't cutting it for me. They had such cute little personalities. Seeing as how I had no idea if they were male, female, or one of each, I'd have to make their nicknames something that could work for either. It seemed like a fun little project to let my brain rest from all the other serious problems I needed to solve.

Shutting and locking the back door behind me, I stood in the kitchen debating whether I wanted to put the effort into making something to eat. All I'd had so far was the lunch I'd packed and a bottle of water, and my body desperately needed the sustenance. But I didn't know if I had the energy to spare for cooking.

I decided on a compromise. I needed to eat, but only if I could find something that just needed to be popped into the microwave for a minute. Rooting around for leftovers in the fridge, I didn't hear my mom come in.

"Well, well, well. Look who decided to return."

Smacking my head on the upper shelf as I jerked at the sudden intrusion, I peered up and over the fridge door. Rubbing my head, I sighed. My mother had become quite surly since we had been staying at the sanctuary. Since her sister had just died, I did try to cut her some slack, but it was beginning to grate on my nerves.

"Well, hello to you too." I tenderly felt the lump that was already forming and sighed.

Silence greeted me. Pushing the fridge door shut, I came out empty-handed. My mother's attitude had killed my appetite.

"Look, I told you I would be gone most of the day. I didn't just take off and disappear with no warning."

"That doesn't mean I wouldn't worry! You didn't even take your phone with you. What if there was an emergency?"

"I didn't take it because I figured I wouldn't get service out in the woods. I'm sorry if you worried."

She harrumphed, not even bothering to answer me. Pushing past me, she began to rustle around in the kitchen cabinets, setting things out on the counter as she went.

"Why don't you go take a shower while I make us some dinner?"

"I think I just want to go to bed and get some sleep. I'm exhausted."

"You look like you could use a meal."

Nodding, I grabbed some pain reliever and headed for the bathroom. She wasn't wrong. The exertion from earlier made me sweaty and sticky, and I doubted I smelled very nice. The hot water would soothe my aching muscles and then I could have a good meal before bed, which hopefully would mediate the worst of the price I'd be paying tomorrow.

The shower ran hot while I lay in the bottom of the tub, letting the water fill it up. Getting over the edge without falling had been a chore in and of itself, making me thankful I had the tub walls to support me when the time to stand up came. While the heat had relaxed my muscles somewhat, they were now achy and refusing to obey the instructions from my brain.

Dressed in sweats and cozy slippers, I hobbled down the hall to the kitchen where my mom silently sat food on the table. She nodded at me as I entered, but didn't speak. The chicken alfredo and garlic bread she put out made me salivate, reigniting the hunger from earlier.

My body demanded I feed it, immediately. I ate more than I could normally ever dream of fitting in my stomach, thankful for the stretchy waistband of the sweatpants I had on.

"Mom. Talk to me. I know your sister just died, but you seem so far from yourself since we've been here. I don't know what to do."

"There isn't much to talk about. You already said it. My sister just died. Apparently I'm not handling it very well. I'd prefer to just pack up and go home, but you seem to want to stay, and I don't think I'm ready to leave you here alone yet. I'd be too worried about losing you too. So I'm doing the best I can. I'm sorry if that isn't good enough for you."

"That's not why I asked. It's not about being good enough for me. But you seem to forget that I am a human being who is also capable of worrying about the ones I love. I just wanted to be sure that you were as okay as you could be, based on the circumstances. If you aren't, I wish you would talk to me about it. That's all. I miss Aunt Aimee too. I also loved her and am struggling to cope with her sudden loss."

For a moment she didn't respond, and I wondered if she was angry. Then she sighed, and a tear slipped down her face. While part of me was shocked and concerned, because she had never been one to show her emotions regularly, the other part of me was glad that she was going to let some of it out.

My suspicions said she had a lot of unresolved guilt over her relationship with Aunt Aimee, and now there was no time left for her to make amends. We both harbored our own guilt, for different reasons, and needed to come to terms with it before we would ever fully be able to heal and move on. My aunt's death left a huge hole in our lives; she had been our only other living relative, and now it truly was just my mom and I together in the world. As cranky as she'd been acting lately, I knew I needed to cut her some slack. She was my only flesh and blood on this earth.

At least I knew Aunt Aimee loved me, and we had been on good terms when she passed. My mom didn't even have that. Of course they still loved each other, but their last words had been in anger, as far as I knew. I couldn't imagine being in Mom's shoes right now.

"I'm sorry, Mom. We are both struggling right now. I'm exhausted, and need to get some sleep. You should probably try to do the same. I'll see you in the morning for breakfast. I love you."

Her eyes searched my face for a minute before she responded. "I love you too, Leah. I always will. No matter what happens here."

I lay in bed, wondering at her cryptic remark. What did she expect to happen here that might make me think her love would change? Sleep claimed me before I had the chance to make any sense of it, giving way to dreams of my aunt, wolves and magic.

CHAPTER ELEVEN

Four o'clock comes right early in the morning when dreams plague every moment of your night. Tired of fighting to banish the fear and unease, I decided getting up for the day was my best option. I needed coffee, and maybe to bake something. Baking soothed my nerves whenever I got frazzled, and I hadn't made Aunt Aimee's chocolate chip cookies in what seemed like forever.

Not bothering to change out of my pajamas, I headed straight for the coffee pot in the kitchen. As I passed by the main room, I noticed a lamp burning.

Detouring to turn it off, I discovered my mother, sitting on the rug in front of the fire place, with boxes surrounding her.

"Mom? What are you doing up? Have you been to sleep at all?"

"I tried. For about three hours. But after dozing fitfully, I figured I might as well just get up; I can always take a nap later. And if I don't hopefully, I'll be tired enough to actually sleep tonight."

"I'm going to put on some coffee and I'll be right back."

Aside from a brief nod, she gave no other indication that she heard me, once again engrossed in whatever she had found in the boxes. My curiosity deepened. While I waited for the coffee to brew, I stared out the window into the forest. The moonlight didn't reach past the clearing, as usual, but that didn't stop my imagination from running wild.

The peninsula had been reserved for the sanctuary in its entirety. It covered vast amounts of land, as well as different ecosystems. The ocean surrounded it on all three sides, of course. In the Northeast corner, a small mountain range sported a single high peak and numerous smaller ones. Rainforest covered much of the mountain's lower altitudes. Spread across the rest of the land lay a vast forest, interrupted only by the small villages where the packs made their homes.

My aunt had always talked of the variety of wildlife that remained protected here, not just the wolves. Knowing what I knew now, I wondered how many of them were shifters too. Some? Most? None? Or all of them?

The little chipmunks I had come to think of as my friends, what about them? I made a mental note to ask Isaiah the next time we got together, which would hopefully be soon. If they turned out to be humans stuck in rodent bodies, I wouldn't feel nearly so ridiculous about talking to them and trying to make friends. On the other hand, if they weren't...

The coffee pot beeped, announcing it was finished with its job and pulling me out of my reverie. Pouring two cups and doctoring them to each of our tastes, I made my way back into the living room where my mom still sat on the floor, surrounded by boxes and what looked like books.

I handed Mom a cup. "Here. I thought you could use some. What are you looking at?"

She reached into the box closest to her and pulled

out a handful of photographs. "Pictures. Aimee loved pictures and took them of everything. There are some as old as when we were in grade school. Obviously they're ones she collected from someone else."

She held one up, showing two smiling little girls wearing matching dresses, hair done in pigtails. They stood in front of a house I didn't recognize, with a small dog at their feet.

"That's you and Aunt Aimee? How old were you?"

She chuckled. "That's us. I was probably about five, which means Aimee was almost seven or so. The dog's name was Teddy." After ruffling through the box some more, she came up with another one. "Here we are on Aimee's tenth birthday. She asked for a crystal ball that year."

"Well? Did she get it?" I reached out and took the photo from her hand, wanting to study it more closely.

Mom's brow furrowed as she thought back. "I don't remember. It was so long ago now."

We rifled through the box, my mom telling stories and me asking questions as we went along. Flipping through the pictures, I noticed they were only of the two of them in the majority of the shots. Very few friends or family had any representation.

"Why aren't there any pictures of grandma or grandpa? Or any aunts and uncles? I haven't seen a single one."

She stopped digging through the box, quiet for a moment. Then she said flippantly, "Your grandmother never wanted to be in the pictures. And your grandfather just wasn't around enough I guess."

Both of them had died before I was born, I assumed, and neither Aimee nor my mother ever had much to say about them. It wasn't a forbidden subject, but one you could tell made them both very uncomfortable.

Pulling the next box over closer, she undid the flaps and pulled out an album that sat on top. Once opened, she gave a little gasp at its contents. Since she didn't make a move to share, I scooted closer so that I could see.

It was full of wedding pictures. Aunt Aimee's wedding pictures, from the looks of it.

"Whatever happened to her husband? My uncle? The look so happy together, yet I never heard her say much about him."

After inhaling deeply, and letting it out slowly, she let the album rest against her legs and finally looked me straight in the eyes.

"Your Uncle Rick disappeared less than a month after the wedding. They went on their honeymoon to Europe, then came back and settled into this house. Not even a week later he went out into the forest to go fishing in the stream and never returned. They searched for him for days. Even some people from town came through and searched the forest."

"Did they ever find any clues at all?"

"None. He vanished without a trace. She even tried using her so-called magic spells to find him." She shook her head. "Aimee used to claim he was a werewolf and could change into an actual wolf. She actually suspected he was with one of the packs somewhere." My mother laughed harshly. "Can you believe it?"

I weighed my words carefully before speaking. "And how do you know she wasn't telling the truth? Aunt Aimee never seemed like that type, the kind to make up wild stories just for the hell of it."

She scoffed. "Leah, please. Have you ever met a human that could turn itself into an animal? Let's be realistic here. That's even more far-fetched than the idea of magical spells and such."

"What if Aunt Aimee was right and magic does exist? You might be able to do magic too, after all, the two of you are closely related. What would it hurt to try? You saw me do it."

"That's preposterous. And I'd appreciate it if you didn't bring it up again. I realize that you are your own person now, and you can believe in whatever nonsense you so choose. I, on the other hand, prefer only to believe in things that make sense. People turning into animals does *not* make any sense."

After finishing her sentence, my mother replaced the album in the box and stood up. Her pursed lips announced without a word that I had taken it too far and she no longer wanted to continue the conversation.

"I think I can finally get some sleep now. You're welcome to continue looking through the boxes. Many of the photos have at least the dates written on the back." She tossed that last sentence back over her shoulder as she stalked down the hall and out of sight.

Frustrated at her lack of open-mindedness, I grabbed a few more albums and flipped through them. Aunt Aimee had gotten married when I was about four years old. While I had no memories of the wedding itself, or actually meeting this Uncle Rick, plenty of pictures provided the proof that I had, indeed, been there. As a flower girl, even.

With a sigh, I studied one of the close ups of the two of them together. Was Aunt Aimee's husband still alive out there somewhere? And if so, would I be able to find him? He'd be much older now, and probably look different, but I figured I'd be able to recognize him if our paths ever crossed. I slipped one of the wedding photos into my pocket, intending to ask Isaiah if he'd ever seen him the next time we got together.

Putting the photos back, I wandered to the kitchen to bake some cookies from Aunt Aimee's favorite recipe. We'd always made them together, and the process helped me to organize my thoughts. Questions without answers swirled around in my head as I measured and mixed.

Something had happened to her husband. The question was, what? The correlation between him heading to the stream which we now knew was the source of a curse upon all the shifters, and his disappearance was way too connected to just be a coincidence. I didn't know where the curse fit into the timeline of the wedding, though.

It broke my heart to think Aunt Aimee had been living with the consequences of this curse for so long. Once again, I wondered whether the two of us would have been able to work together to reverse it long before now.

She must have known about the other pack Isaiah had mentioned, though. She knew everything about the sanctuary, or so I had always assumed. She would have looked there if she thought she would find him.

Isaiah would have been a small child, like me, when Rick disappeared, but maybe someone in his pack knew of the situation. Aunt Aimee had talked to the pack, so if they knew something they likely would have told her. Even if it didn't lead to finding him, it would still be more information than I currently had.

Once I ate breakfast and packed most of the cookies I had baked, I called out to Isaiah and headed down the trail. He answered that he was already on his way and would see me in just a minute.

"What are you doing out and about so early?" He walked around the corner, very human and very handsome.

Just seeing him made me smile. "I couldn't sleep, so I got up at four o'clock and came downstairs to find my mother looking through boxes and boxes of Aunt Aimee's old photos that she found. Including her wedding albums."

I watched him for a moment to see if that triggered anything for him. Nope. "That sounds like fun," was his only response.

"Yeah, but it gave me more questions than answers."

I relayed every detail about my uncle's disappearance that my mom had given me and pulled the photo from my backpack. I asked him if he knew anything about it, or recognized my uncle.

Head shaking, he reached around and rubbed the back of his neck. "Some of our older members might know, and I can ask them. There is a smaller pack on the East side of the reserve, situated in the foothills of the mountain range. It's possible he somehow ended up there. Technically, though, he would belong to my pack, because his house is here, and this is his territory."

"So, there are more wolves? For some reason I thought your pack was the only one, although my aunt often talked about other animals that lived in the safety of the sanctuary."

"Yes, there are others. The sanctuary is a home to both shifters and normal woodland creatures. The magic that protects the land here keeps our kind hidden, should anyone wander out into the forest and come upon us. Our elders say the other pack is made up of not just wolves, but a variety of shifters who didn't have a family or group when they came to these lands to settle here."

"How far is it to the other territory? Could we go there at some point?"

"Our two packs usually stay on our own sides of the sanctuary, but I might be able to arrange a visit. Not today, though. And it's a fairly long way to walk, which is our only mode of transportation available because of the terrain. It would probably take at least five hours for you to walk it. Even as my wolf I couldn't carry you."

Once more the thought of being in such close contact with him had my cheeks heating up. My imagination ran wild as I thought of clenching my thighs against him. I laughed to hide my embarrassment. "I would never expect you to carry me!"

"I wouldn't mind."

The statement sent shivers down my spine. Raising my eyes to meet his, I found him watching me already. My cheeks flamed even more. Stupid hormones. Maybe I could look up a spell to douse them in frigid water every time they threatened to get out of control. If I was going to practice witchcraft, I should at least learn something useful.

"You might change your tune once you find out how heavy I am." I raised my eyebrows in a teasing challenge.

"Oh yeah? You think so? I think not."

Before I could answer, he reached out and snatched me up as if I were no more than a doll, tossing me over his shoulder in a fireman's carry. I sucked in my breath as I realized it gave me the perfect vantage point to admire his ass, all while giggling uncontrollably. I clenched my fist to keep from reaching down and pinching his denim-clad cheeks.

His hands splayed across the backs of my legs, the warmth of them burning through my jeans and making me aware of exactly their size and shape as they kept me from falling. His fingertips just brushed the sensitive area at the inside of my thighs. My self-control was fast disappearing.

I swatted at him, demanding to be put down as he began striding down the trail. "You can't just carry me around like a piece of furniture!"

"Well, it looks to me like I can, actually." His hands tightened on my legs, giving them a gentle squeeze.

The sensation almost made me forget how to breathe.

"Where are we going? This is kidnapping. You can't do this."

"I believe it's only kidnapping if the person doesn't want to go."

"Maybe I don't?" The temptation to sink my teeth into him was going to get the better of me if he didn't put me down soon, and then we'd really find ourselves in a situation.

"Yes, you do. Trust me."

"If you don't put me down, I am going to bite you. I'm not kidding."

His laughter shook me even more than his walking did. "Go ahead, sassy pants. Just remember, I bite back."

I choked on my response. Did I dare? I wanted to so badly. But I barely knew him. What was I thinking? On the other hand, he practically invited me to do it. Maybe he wanted me to? Was that a challenge? Because I had never been one to back down from a challenge. Before I could make up my mind, he grabbed my waist and swung me back upright, setting me gently on the ground.

I'd missed my chance. Shit. Damn it. Fuck.

Something told me leaning over and biting him now wouldn't have nearly the same effect.

"I thought we could go to the village, and I'd take you to meet the rest of my pack. I've told them about you, and maybe we can get some of your questions answered."

CHAPTER TWELVE

Meet his pack? His family and friends and the people he was in charge of keeping safe? Was I ready for this? What would they think of me? What if they didn't like me?

"Hello? Earth to Leah?"

"Oh! Yeah. I mean, yes?"

"Are you okay with that? Do you want to go and meet the rest of the pack? Maybe get to know some of them a little bit?"

"Today? Like, now?"

He burst out laughing. "Did you need to check your schedule? Should I make an appointment for later this week? I know you've been incredibly busy these last couple days."

Swatting him lightly on the arm, I couldn't help but grin. My concern, however, tempered the grin. "I'm not dressed for this. I didn't even really do my hair this morning. What if they don't like me?"

"Why wouldn't they love you? Besides, I have a surprise for them. Nobody else knows I have my ability to shift back. Once I show them that it is possible, and they know you are the one responsible for this miracle, they will adore you."

"Oh God... What if I can't do it for them? It took everything I had to do it for you, and that was with all your strength helping me. Then they'll hate me."

"Leah." He threw his arm around my shoulder and pulled me close. "They won't hate you. You helped me the hard way, by forcing it. When you manage to reverse the curse, they will all get their ability to shift back, and they will love you for it. I know they will."

Still, I hesitated. Insecurity raised its ugly head, hammering into me. Unsure of why I cared so much what they thought of me, I just somehow knew that if they didn't accept me, it would be infinitely harder to do the things I needed to do for the sanctuary. They knew my aunt and loved her. The need to make her proud settled deep within me. Which I couldn't do if I avoided the community she dedicated almost her entire life to serving and protecting.

"Okay. Let's do this."

"You sound like you think I am about to throw you into an active volcano." He stopped walking and looked into my eyes. "We don't have to if you don't want to."

"No, I want to. I'm just incredibly nervous for some reason." I inhaled sharply. "What they think of me is important to me. Usually the opinions of others don't matter to me. At all. But, this sanctuary and those who live here were my Aunt's life work. She died trying to make things right for them. I don't want to let her, or you, or them, down."

He grabbed my hand and began walking down the trail once more. "Look at all you have already done for me. You could never let me down. And we both know Aimee is incredibly proud of you already, no matter what happens here. Nothing you could do would change that. As for the pack, they may be disappointed if you can't help them, but they would understand. This curse, and the evil that has perpetuated it, is so strong. But I know you can do it. I can feel it. You have the crescent mark. The sanctuary *chose* you."

Pulling my hand from his grasp, I turned it over and stared at the mark on my palm. The odd combination of birthmark and scar stood out against my pale flesh. Isaiah seemed to understand that I needed some quiet time to soothe my thoughts.

"I am going to return to my wolf form so we can surprise them."

I stared at him. "Should I turn my back?"

He laughed. "It's not like getting naked, you can watch if you want."

The thought of seeing him naked made my face flame. I seemed to blush more often than usual when I spent time with him. Our eyes met, and he winked. As I watched the air around him seemed to waver, and he folded in upon himself. One second he stood before me on two legs, and in the next his dark gray wolf had replaced him. We continued to walk as I processed what I had just seen.

Time passed as we traversed the trail, Isaiah answering my questions as they came to mind. From one step to the next, the mark began to ache and itch, stopping me in my tracks. This only happened when magic was nearby. I look around at the forest, seeing nothing.

Isaiah stopped next to me. "What's wrong?"

"My mark, it's aching. That means there is magic nearby."

He nodded. "We are at the border of the village."

My eyebrows raised. I saw no village. Or anything but trees, for that matter.

"Our homes are hidden by an illusion. Once you cross the border for the first time, it will no longer be hidden to you, but it is to protect us. To all outsiders the peninsula looks to be devoid of any inhabitation, aside from your aunt's home, whether they come by air, land or sea. Watch."

He leaned against me for a second, my hand resting on his back, the contact soothing the ache in the mark. Together we walked another thirty feet and suddenly stood at the edge of a small cluster of homes and buildings. My feet once more refused to keep moving as I stared at the scene in front of me.

The wolves in view all sat or stood staring our direction. My nerves returned tenfold. I heard him call out to the pack in my head, asking all of them to meet us at the central park. As we approached it, I saw a wide expanse of lawn, perfect for gatherings. Isaiah led me to the center while we waited for the others to join us. I felt like a goldfish in a bowl.

He somehow knew when everyone had joined us and began to speak.

"All of you knew Aimee. This is her niece, Leah, whom I have been speaking of to you recently. Leah has come to help us rid the sanctuary of the evil that has plagued our pack for years."

Snippets of the conversations among the wolves registered in my head, but I was unable to catch all of it. Some of the wolves sounded excited. Others did not believe that I had any chance of helping them. Isaiah gave them a minute to talk before continuing.

"I know there are some of you who do not believe she is capable. I disagree. To that end I would like to share something with you. Something that may change your mind."

He waited for complete silence before looking at me one last time. My breath caught in my chest as I waited. Again I watched the air wrinkle around him and he stood before me in his human form once more. The cacophony of disbelief was instantaneous and deafening.

Isaiah took my hand as the wolves left their positions and began to crowd around us. The din in my head of their conversations was overwhelming. Suddenly, a snarl came from our left.

Turning towards the angry wolf that stalked toward us, Isaiah tugged me closer, putting himself between the black animal and me. "Adam, what is the problem here?"

The other wolves stared at him, some seeming to be on his side. While we waited for a response Isaiah informed me that Adam was his beta, what the wolves called the second in command.

"How do we know she is not the one who created this evil? That would make it easy for her to remove it just for you. What proof do you have that we can trust her?"

My legs turned to jello at the idea that some of them thought I might be responsible for the terrible things that had been happening. Of all my concerns in coming to meet the pack, that one had never crossed my mind.

Adam continued to snarl as he advanced our way. "I will not accept that you choose to endanger our pack by bringing her into our midst."

Isaiah stood tall. "That is enough. She damn near killed herself doing it, and that was with all my alpha power behind her trying to help." He took a deep breath and tempered his tone. "While I understand some of you are wary, and rightfully so, I will not tolerate you accusing her of being the evil. Would you be making these accusations if Aimee stood before you by her side? Aimee gave her life trying to help us, and this is how you would treat her niece, who came to attempt to finish what her aunt started?"

Many of the wolves murmured in agreement, some hanging their heads sheepishly. Others moved through the crowd to stand near the wolf called Adam. I heard a number of apologies given. I also heard other grumbles about whether Isaiah was fit to lead if he was so easily convinced to trust an outsider.

The power in Isaiah's voice flowed over me as he began to speak again. "As your alpha, it is both my right and my duty to make decisions for this pack. While I will never try to tell you who to trust, I will ask that you give her a chance. You should all know that she is under my protection. If any of you would like to challenge that, you are welcome to do so now."

His eyes bored into Adam's as he spoke. The other

wolf struggled to meet his gaze, but was unable to hold it. Refusing to look at the ground in submission, he turned and looked out into the houses as Isaiah sighed.

"I will not remain beta to an alpha who cannot place his pack above his own gain. I'm done here."

Adam loped off, four others following him as they left the village the opposite way of where we had come in. Guilt swamped me again, but Isaiah squeezed my hand and used our private communication path to tell me not to worry about it, that he would deal with it later.

On the community channel he issued an invitation. "Those of you who wish to come and get to know Leah, please do. She would love the chance to get to know you as well."

A small group turned and left the lawn without acknowledging me. Others came up and introduced themselves, many expressing sorrow at losing my aunt. I apologized ahead of time that many of them would have to tell me their names more than once for them to stick.

"I'm just terrible at remembering names, I'm so sorry. It's one of those things that I haven't been able to cure about myself."

For those that stuck around, I gave them a brief

version of what had happened since we came to the sanctuary, answering what questions I could and doing my best to reassure them that I would do everything in my power to help them.

Sometime later Isaiah asked if I was ready to go. "There's some place I'd like to take you if you're up for it?"

We said our goodbyes to the rest of the pack, and I promised to return soon. One of the females stayed behind for an extra minute. Her name was Shelby.

"Thank you. For everything you've done so far. I hope when you come back we can get to know each other better; I'd love to be friends."

Hope bloomed. "I would love that. I really would."

She loped away as Isaiah began leading me away from the settlement. "That didn't go as badly as I had expected. Except for the one guy."

He gave me a grin. "I told you. Although I'm sorry not all of them were welcoming. Adam will come around. I have no doubt he'll come back to talk to me and we can work it out. If not, that's his choice."

We talked as we walked, Isaiah telling me more about pack life and how the evil had affected every aspect of life within the sanctuary. The pack always believed the magic that created the sanctuary had been the strongest in existence, so when the evil was able to take over many of them were left hopeless.

There had been no births since the curse, since wolf shifters gave birth to human infants that then learned to shift as they matured. My heart broke for them. The wolves believed in a goddess that protected them, and many of them had lost their faith when their pleas for help went unanswered.

"Our homes have been protected all this time, never changing in spite of the fact that we can no longer maintain them the way we did before, and we remain hidden from the outside world, but for some reason the Goddess cannot overcome the curse."

Struggling with the idea that I needed to do something even a goddess could not, I said a prayer of my own for the strength I would need to be successful. My thoughts were interrupted by Isaiah telling me to close my eyes.

I glanced at him before doing as he asked. He led me by the hand, repeating to keep my eyes closed until he told me to open them. Of course, as was my way, I tripped over absolutely nothing, thankful he managed to keep me upright. After walking blindly for a length of the trail, he tugged me to a stop.

"Okay, open them."

We stood at the edge of a sandy beach. The tiny cove mimicked the shape of the crescent moon, protecting the little bay from the rougher ocean waters, explaining why I hadn't heard waves crashing. They simply rolled up to the shore.

"Oh my gosh, I love it. It's so beautiful." I threw my arms around him. "Thank you."

He hugged me back, the feeling of his arms around me driving away my uncertainties. It felt so safe to be cradled in his embrace.

"Come here. This isn't the only surprise."

He led me down the beach a short way. Driftwood had been piled to create a seating area, complete with a fire pit ringed by stones. With delighted laughter I called for flames, a spell I had mastered early on, and lit our fire.

"This is so perfect." Shrugging off my backpack, I rooted around inside it. "I actually brought you a surprise too, and they go perfectly together."

From the pack I pulled the large container of cookies and two individual sized bottles of sparkling cider, another of mine and Aunt Aimee's favorites.

Finding them in the pantry had brought a smile to my face.

We settled in against the logs, talking and snacking, taking the opportunity to learn about each other. We sat close enough that our legs, stretched out in front of us, pressed together. The hours passed in what seemed like minutes.

The sun had passed over our heads and begun to sink toward the horizon. "I probably need to get you home, huh?"

"As much as I hate to say it, probably. I don't relish the idea of a long walk through the woods in the dark."

"Well, we actually aren't far from your house. We came by a very roundabout route, but the walk back should only be about twenty or thirty minutes."

The news surprised me. I'd be able to come here again. Hopefully with him, and hopefully soon. Making sure we had our trash and the cookie container, I took one last look at the ocean and extinguished the fire. Isaiah got to his feet, extending his hand to pull me up.

He gave a little extra tug, causing me to stumble and lose my balance, falling into him. My hands splayed across his chest, and I reveled in the feeling of his muscles beneath my palms. "You did that on purpose!"

Our eyes met. "Would you blame me if I did?"

For a moment, neither of us spoke. The gentle noise of the water was the only sound, aside from both of our labored breathing. Praying for a kiss, I shivered in disappointment as he pulled me in for a hug instead.

"Leah." The way he said my name made my knees weak and my panties wet.

"Yes?" The word barely squeezed past my lips.

"Thank you for today." He released me, stepping back to look at my face once more. "I can't tell you how much this day meant to me. All of it. I hope we get to do this more often."

"Me too."

We made our way home in relative silence. I spent the time pondering how to best help him and his pack. The closer we got to each other, the more determined I became. This was a man I wanted in my life.

Arriving back at the house, we stopped just short of the clearing. "Here you are, my lady. Safe and sound." He looked up at the house. "I meant what I said at the beach. I want to spend more time with you. I hope you decide to stay even after the curse is broken. Will you think about it?"

My heart clenched. Words failed me, and I nodded

instead of speaking. The nod brought a smile to his face as he lifted my hand to his lips.

"See you soon."

CHAPTER THIRTEEN

Instead of going directly inside, I settled down in the swing on the back porch. My eyes drifted closed as I thought of the day I'd just had. My feelings for Isaiah crept forward, taking over my other thoughts. They scared me a little. I'd been attracted to him before I even knew what he "really" looked like.

My wandering thoughts got interrupted by tiny scratches on the back of my hand, followed by rapid-fire chattering. The two little chipmunks that I'd been seeing around were back, probably for more crackers.

They took turns chattering and running in circles, down off the table onto the wooden porch and back again.

"Hey guys. Are you hungry again?" I realized I had forgotten to ask Isaiah if there was a way I could identify shifters from normal woodland creatures.

More chattering and running amok. Unable to speak chipmunk, I stood up, intending to get them some crackers, when they both ran off the porch and then looked back, as if to see whether I would follow them. Shrugging, I began to go after them when my mom poked her head out the back door.

"What are you doing out here?"

Pointing in the direction of my little friends, I answered her. "I'll be right back. They want me to follow them."

"Seriously, Leah? You think you should follow rodents out into the forest after dark? Where is your brain?"

A glance at the sky brought me to my senses. It was indeed close to complete darkness. More time must have passed while I daydreamed than I had realized. Had I dozed off?

"You're right. I wasn't thinking."

Unhappy chatter came from the pair as they raced

the rest of the way across the clearing and up a nearby tree. Their little clicks and squeaks followed me into the house, igniting my curiosity about where they wanted me to go and what they could possibly want to show me.

My stomach growled at the smell of the food simmering in the kitchen. Yes, we'd eaten the entire batch of cookies, but that did not make a meal. Since I planned to work on my magic, I needed more substantial nutrition to keep me going. Thankfully, Mom had been in a cooking mood and the scent of chicken parmigiana wafted through the air.

She brushed by me to remove the garlic knots from the oven. She made them from scratch and I could eat a dozen at a time they were so good. While she served plates, I grabbed silverware, napkins and drinks. We sat down to eat in companionable silence. At first.

Mom cleared her throat. "So, what did you do all day?"

Indecision flooded me. My desire to be honest with her warred with my instinct to avoid conflict. Something told me she wouldn't be thrilled with my answer if I told her everything that had gone on while I'd been away from the house.

I tried to deflect the question. "Not much. What did

you do?"

"Nice try, Leah."

Failure on the first attempt. Deciding to go on the offensive, I followed with another question of my own. "Would you believe me if I told you? Or would you make fun of me and act like I'm losing my marbles?"

"Le-ah..." She drew out the syllables of my name in exasperation.

"Mom. You can't blame me for asking. You keep denying the existence of magic, in spite of seeing me do it with your own eyes. You refuse to even open your mind and accept the possibility that things outside our realm of experience do exist. On top of that you are kind of a brat when I do talk about it."

"I just think you are a little old to be indulging in such fantasies. That's all."

My irritation got the better of me and I stood, my appetite deserting me. Carrying my plate to the sink, I bit out my response. "Don't continue to ask me about my activities until you are willing to listen without judgment. I know you aren't blind or stupid. So, that leaves one other scenario. What are you afraid of?"

Ignoring her pleas to stay and talk, I stalked out through the doorway and upstairs to the door at the end of the hall, slamming it behind me as I made my way back into the attic. It still contained so many books that I hadn't even cracked open yet. There could be anything in the stacks of unopened boxes. The wealth of knowledge contained there beckoned me. The answers I needed had to be hiding up there somewhere, just waiting to be found.

Choosing one of the older volumes, I began reading. It contained notes about creating spells, not just using ones that had been passed down by the generations before. From my understanding, it took great power to create an incantation that would harness the power needed for others to be able to use it after it had been perfected. Some of them appeared to do things I never believed possible.

The passage that caught my attention first related to borrowing power from the world around you. The spidery handwriting spoke of ley lines, and the power contained within mother Earth herself. Instructions on finding those sources of power and tapping into them covered the page. It took only moments for me to learn the feeling of reaching out and finding the power around me.

The author ended the passage with warnings not to

overdo it. Each witch had the capability to borrow the power, but individuals had very different capacities for storing and using it. Trying to go above and beyond your capacity for magic would hurt you rather than help you.

The deterrent language caused me to shrug. How could I possibly know my limitations if I didn't attempt to go beyond them, at least a little bit? With a reasonably cautious mindset, I reached out to the world around, asking politely to borrow the power I wished to make use of. The gentle flow filled me like a chalice, giving me more oomph than I had learned to use from my own body.

Fatigue began to set in as I alternated reading about magic and the history of the sanctuary and practicing the spells I ran across in the books. Frustrated at my inability to master one of the skills I had chosen, I held my breath, pulling as much power to myself as I could muster. Instead of the result I'd expected, a bright light flashed before me, the accompanying boom rattling my senses.

Opening my eyes, I found myself far from the attic, seemingly alone in a land shrouded in mist and fog. Towering trees loomed over me, making me wonder if I found myself somewhere within the boundaries of the sanctuary. Instead of being scared, however, I felt peaceful. Wherever I had landed, the evil had not yet reached that place.

But where was I, and how the hell had I gotten myself here? I hadn't been trying to leave the attic. The spell hadn't been one of transportation, although I'd seen one within the pages. Soft, raspy whispers reached my ears. At first, I couldn't make out the words, just the murmuring voice. The closer it came, the clearer the words became.

"Hello?" Nobody appeared to be approaching, yet I felt clearly that I was no longer alone.

"You must find them..."

Spinning in a slow circle, I looked for the source of the voice. "Find what?"

"Find the pages. They hold the key."

"The journal pages? Where are they?" As I asked the question I moved to the edge of the clearing, trying to explore further, but I couldn't leave the immediate area. The mist acted as a barrier.

"Find them."

"Find them."

"Find them."

Other voices began to chime in. Unidentifiable,

disembodied whispers chimed in from every direction.

"Where are they? Where should I look? I don't know where to start!"

"You know how to find them. You must hurry. Time is running out. Find the pages."

"How do I get back? I can't find anything if I'm stuck here with no way home."

The voices faded away, leaving me alone in the silence. Walking the perimeter of the clearing enforced my assumption that I couldn't leave the small space I found myself in. Aggravation swamped me. I attempted to slam my palm against the barrier, but my hand went right through. It could keep me from walking through, but did not have a physical presence I could reach out and touch.

Eyes closing, I sank to the floor of the forest. I needed to focus. Holding the picture of the attic in my mind, I attempted to will myself back there. While I'd seen the transportation spell in the book, I'd considered it outside my current abilities and hadn't attempted it. I'd read over the notes, though, and knew you had to keep your destination firmly in mind.

Sometime later, I felt a hand on my shoulder. "Keep your eyes closed."

Startled, I struggled to obey. The pressure comforted me, rather than alarming me, and I managed to not look.

"Curses are nothing more than a tight knot. Some of them are more complicated than others, but all of them follow the same construct. As you unravel the knots, you will begin to remove the power from the curse. Untie the knots..." The voice trailed off.

I began to shake, feeling as if my head might explode at any minute.

"Leah! Leah!" More shaking. "Leah, can you hear me, honey?"

"Argh." A groan was all I could manage at first. "Stop yelling at me."

"Oh my, thank the goddess."

With concerted effort, I managed to pry my eyelids open. My mom's tear-stained face swam into focus.

"Mom? Why are you crying?" Struggling, I tried to sit up.

"Wait just a minute, sweetie. Don't try to get up yet."

"I'm okay." I ignored her, paying for it with the dizziness that swamped me as I made it upright. "What happened?"

Sticky wetness flowed down onto my upper lip. Before even touching my face, I knew that my efforts to increase the amount of magic I could use had caused a bloody nose once more. Mom pushed the already crimson-covered dish towel at my face.

"What were you doing up here? There was a large bang, and I came running up here to find you laying on the floor. Your nose just kept bleeding and no matter what, I couldn't rouse you. Then you started mumbling, so I knew you hadn't died, but I couldn't get you to wake up. I thought I was going to lose you. I almost went down to call an ambulance."

"Ah, Mom, I'm sorry. I think I might have been attempting to operate above my pay grade. I'm fine. I'll be okay, I promise."

"You've got to stop this! You are going to kill yourself."

"Mom, I think while I was unconscious Aunt Aimee came to me. She was talking to me and telling me to find her journal pages."

"Aimee is dead. She was not here to talk to you. You must have been dreaming. You hit your head hard enough when you fell to addle your brain cells."

"Ugh. Okay. I'm sorry I scared you. I think I need to

get downstairs and get some sleep. What time is it?"

"Almost midnight."

"Midnight? How long was I out?"

"About thirty minutes."

I'd been practicing before passing out for much longer than I had expected. I'd also been up for almost twenty hours straight. My body needed to recharge. Desperately.

With Mom's help, I managed to get to my feet. Leaving the books right where they lay, we headed down the steep staircase. I'd be back to get the pile once I got some sleep, knowing they held more information that I needed.

Standing before the bathroom mirror as I washed the evidence of my nose bleed down the sink, I stared at my reflection. On top of flecks of dried blood, deep purple bags had formed beneath my eyes. My lips, usually so rosy, faded to a pale apricot. They looked dry and cracked. Even my eyes were dull and lifeless. A few hours of good solid sleep would hopefully restore my vigor.

If it didn't, I didn't know how I would manage to continue attempting to remove the curse. It would take every ounce of strength I could muster to be successful.

Continuing to drive myself to this level of weakness would leave me vulnerable, both unable to protect myself and inadequately prepared to untie the knots in the curse and restore the pack's memories and abilities to shift.

My mind replayed the scene in in the vision, or whatever it had been. Forest was forest and trees were trees, so I didn't attempt to identify a particular clearing. What I did want to know is whether it had truly been my aunt who came to me while I was there. Nobody else that I knew of would have much of an interest in whether or not I found the missing journal pages, and I didn't think there would be anyone else who even knew what might be on them.

But if it had been her, then why did I need to keep my eyes closed when she touched my shoulder? Why couldn't I see her just one last time?

If I was being honest with myself, the experience seemed to give me more questions than answers. That, however, was only true if I focused on the who and not the what. The piece of information about the curse would hopefully lead me to being able to untangle it.

Maybe more would come to me as I slept.

CHAPTER FOURTEEN

White mist swirled about, thicker than before. It deadened any sounds that might have otherwise reached my ears. Unlike my previous visit to the place I christened Peace, this moment brought me nothing but feelings of impending doom. The crescent mark ached and began to glow, making me wary.

Torn between staying silent and waiting to see what happened, or calling out and risking drawing adverse attention, I crept toward the edge of the clearing. My feet, clad only in socks, made no sound. Wondering if the barrier would hinder me from leaving as before, I reached out to touch the mist. The icy feel of it numbed the skin on my fingers, turning the nail beds blue. Another change.

Curling my fingers inward, I blew my warm breath on them, trying to reverse the effects of instant frostbite. The temperature in the clearing began to drop. My toes, with no shoes to protect them, began to ache.

Suddenly, I heard a voice calling my name. A familiar voice. My ears strained to hear the words that followed. What was Isaiah doing here? I prayed he wasn't in danger, but this place didn't seem like a safe one for a stroll. Was he dreaming too? Or had I somehow sucked him into one of mine?

Deciding to take the risk of drawing unwanted attention, I yelled for him. If he got lost out in the frozen mist, he wouldn't survive for very long. My voice echoed back to me, as if bouncing off the vapor. He couldn't hear me because the invisible barrier affected sound as well.

A shadowy figure became visible through the mist. I screamed his name, but he couldn't hear me, even as he walked right up to the edge of the clearing. To him, the clearing didn't exist. He just kept wandering through the trees, calling my name. The second he walked close enough to come in contact with the perimeter of my temporary cell, I slipped from the dream, waking in a cold sweat in my bed.

My pajamas clung to me like a second skin for what seemed like the hundredth time since I came to the sanctuary. Hair that had escaped the braid was plastered to my neck and forehead. The bedside clock tried insisting that only three minutes had passed since the last time I laid eyes on it. Bullshit. I'd been in that clearing far longer than that.

Limping down the hall to the bathroom, thanks to my aching feet, I slipped into a warm shower in an attempt to defrost myself from the time spent in the dream mist. There would be no sleep for me if I continued to shiver and shake. Leaning my head against the wall, I pondered whether I should reach out to Isaiah through our mental link. My fear was that I'd wake him, and his appearance in my dream had been just that, part of the dream.

Back in my room, I threw on some sweats, undecided about whether to try and sleep again just yet. Settling on a compromise, I crawled under the covers and propped myself up with pillows and one of the books from the attic. Before I got the chance to open it, the crescent mark began to ache, giving off a faint glow. The evil spirit was active.

Feeling a pull stronger than anything I'd experienced so far, I parted the curtains to look out the window. In the distance, approximately in the area of the ruins, a dark cloud formed, growing as I watched. Bolts of lightning crackled among the clouds, sizzling blue instead of the normal yellowish-white.

Shoving my feet into tennis shoes and grabbing a jacket to protect against the chilly night air, I made my way down the stairs and out the back door. The night air crackled with a strange electricity. The hair on my arms stood up under the layers of cotton and my skin crawled. Despite the darkness of the night, my feet found their way along the trail with very few missteps, surprising considering the amount of things I tripped over on a daily basis.

When I reached the edge of the ruins, I paused. Instinctively knowing that the spirit would have far more power once I crossed into its territory, I gathered my strength. Using the lesson from the book, I pulled power from the forest around me, hoping to be prepared for whatever I found on the other side of the stacked stone wall.

"Something strange is going on at the temple..." Throwing a thought to the wind, and hoping Isaiah would hear me, I prepared to make my way inside the building, pausing one more time, thinking I should wait for back up.

From behind me, a vicious growl sounded. I spun on my heel, losing my balance and crashing to the ground. A sleek black wolf crouched less than ten feet from me, canines bared. Attempting to use the same communication method I had established with Isaiah proved futile. Either this particular wolf couldn't hear me, or didn't care.

Inch by inch I returned to a standing position, wracking my brain for a spell that would send the wolf away but not hurt it. It crawled toward me another three feet, its belly almost touching the ground. It hadn't sounded so mean, I would have said it was scared.

"I don't want to hurt you. Go on, get. Shoo."

My feeble attempts failed. Advancing once more, it now stood within striking distance. Once out of the shadows, I could see its body trembling as it prepared to pounce. Figuring that getting inside the temple might be safer than out here trying to avoid being eaten, I half turned to climb over the disintegrating wall.

Taking my eyes off my foe, even for a second, proved disastrous. In the instant I tried to see where I could put my foot on the other side, the beast sprang. Its sharp teeth latched onto my forearm, sending pain shooting up the limb. Instinct kicked in as I slammed my other palm against the side of its head, sending whatever magic I had into the skull.

The animal yelped at the same time I cried out in pain as I ripped my flesh from its teeth. My momentum carried me over the wall, landing hard enough to knock the wind out of me. As I struggled to drag air into my lungs, I could hear the canine on the other side huffing in pain, interspersed with growls.

The second I could breathe, I pulled myself up with my good arm, cradling the bleeding one against my body. Evil spirit or not, I needed to get inside and away from the wolf before the pain of my magic wore off.

The ground under my feet trembled as soon as I was upright; the rumble climbed up my legs and made keeping my balance difficult. Still, I continued through the ruins toward the temple, using the moonlight to avoid the worst of the pitfalls. As soon as my feet left the forest soil and crossed onto the concrete floor, the trembling ceased. Inside, the entry hall was pitch black.

The tiny orb of light that had been my first introduction to magic winked into existence at my request. It provided enough light to make my way forward, but didn't come close to banishing the shadows from the farthest corners of the room.

As I made my way farther into the building, it became apparent that someone, or something, had been inside since the last time I'd been there. The altar where my aunt's body had lain now sat in a crumpled heap, its pieces cascading down the stairs and across the floor. Some of the statues had fallen from, or been knocked from, their pedestals and were nothing more than shards on the stone below.

A wind blew through the chamber, carrying voices to my ears. Whispers, interspersed with shrieks, assaulted my eardrums. No intelligible words could be heard, but the pain and fear needed no words to express itself.

Doing my best to block it out, I reached out with my senses, trying to put the lessons from the book into practice and hoping they would guide me to where I needed to go. Each side of the room had a dark hall leading off of it, and no indication of which would lead me to the spirit. Did I go in the direction the wind came from, or where it led?

"Where are you, damn it?"

As soon as my voice left my throat the wind stopped, and the voices it had been carrying disappeared. The sudden lack of sound startled me.

"Le-ah..." The disembodied voice swirled around me like a tiny cyclone, giving no indication of its origin. "Come here, Leah."

"Where are you hiding, you coward?"

The answering cackle chilled me to the bone. I'd never before had such an evil laugh hit my ears. It scraped against my eardrums like fingernails on a chalkboard, driving the sound into my brain like an ice pick. The sound would be burned into my memories for the rest of my life.

For a brief moment, my little orb of light went dark, leaving me with no sight. When it reappeared, it floated at the entrance to the hallway on my left. Taking the only clue I'd been given so far, I followed it.

The passage led straight to the West, crossing over far more ground than the premises appeared to cover from the outside. No doorways broke the long smooth walls, and no other source of light existed aside from the orb I created. If it went out again, I would have to feel my way back to the entrance and hope nothing nefarious got in my way.

The hall began to spiral, leading down below the surface of the ground. The thought that I should wait for Isaiah, or go back to get help crossed my mind. My magical skills were in no way up to a battle with an evil like I felt here. Turning around, I ran smack into a rough stone wall. My forehead slammed into it, giving me an instant headache. The path back had been blocked. Down was the only option available to me.

Muttering to myself, I continued on. The chill in the air seeped through the layers I wore, giving me goosebumps. My calf muscles began to protest the continued steep grade of the unrelenting path. My only light source grew dimmer as the darkness became more oppressive. This dark was no longer just the absence of light, but a physical force pressing down on me. True fear began to creep into my bones.

As I rounded the curved wall, the faintest hint of blue light came from in front of me, bouncing off the pale stone walls as it crept from around a heavy wooden door. Runes and symbols covered every inch of the available surface. A lump in my pocket grew heavy and warm. Reaching in, I found the iron key I had removed from Aunt Aimee's hand on the day we saw her body. I didn't know how it had gotten there, but I had no doubt it fit the keyhole in the door in front of me.

The key turned in the lock as expected, and I pushed the door open on smooth hinges. In the scary movies doors always creaked when they opened, and for a brief moment I felt let down that this particular scene didn't live up to what lived in my imagination. Once the door no longer blocked my view, I could take in the room in front of me.

The walls and ceiling of the room were covered in the same patterned markings as the door. The stone below my feet gave way to packed dirt just over the threshold. Something stopped me from taking the final step onto the earthen floor.

The blue light brightened in front of me, bringing my attention to the bubble floating in the center of the room. A dark shadow thrashed within the confines of the light. As I watched, it slowed, then stopped altogether, and I could feel its focus turn to me.

The shadow morphed into a human form; the prison confining its changing shape with it. A woman stared at me before beginning to laugh maniacally. The cackle that had found its way to me up above emanated from the gaping mouth. She thrust out her arms, slamming her power into the walls of the spell that contained her. Cracks splintered across its surface.

Her form, although a complete stranger, seemed familiar in a distant sort of way. A sense of having seen her before somewhere, maybe, rippled through me.

She placed both palms on the barrier facing me, pressing against it. My breath caught as the crescent mark on her palm, identical to mine but on the opposite hand, began to glow. Unable to drag my eyes from the shape before me, it took a moment for me to notice that my own mark felt like it caught fire. The burning sensation spread from my palm up my arm.

The voice hissed from her unmoving lips. "You are in way over your head, little girl. You don't even know who I am, do you?"

"That may be so, but I'll be damned if I let you escape." As I spoke I reached for the power I had brought in with me, borrowed from nature and the sanctuary itself.

Her only response was another laugh as she slammed her hands against the containment, widening the cracks. Her power began to seep through them and wind toward me.

"It is only a matter of time until these spells give way. They have been weakening since the moment Aimee died. And once I am free, I will do the same to you as I did to her."

The statement had its intended effect, pain stabbing through my heart at the mention of Aunt Aimee, knowing this creature had killed her. My knees weakened, and I had to grab the wall for support to keep from falling to the floor.

"Aimee thought she could take me on. What an absurd idea!" The spirit almost crooned the words. "I took great pleasure in wrapping my magic around her neck and squeezing the life from her. It wasn't quite as satisfying as using my own two hands, but you don't always get what you want. In spite of being contained here, I could taste her fear. I felt the blackness crawl over her as she struggled to take a breath, unable to drag any air into her lungs."

CHAPTER FIFTEEN

Soft murmurs reached my ears, which stopped as a door latched shut with a click. With great effort, I peeled my eyelids open, blinking at the sudden assault of light against my corneas. As the room around me quit swimming, my focus landed on Isaiah, perched in the chair at my bedside.

"How did I get here? And what are you doing here?" The words hurt my throat.

"I brought you here. I heard your message about something odd happening at the temple, so I headed that way. I tried to tell you to wait for me, but something blocked me. I couldn't get through to you."

"That must have been because I already stepped into the ruins. I could tell something was different as soon as I fell over the wall at the perimeter. A wolf attacked me." Pulling the sleeve up, I examined the bite, which didn't seem to be as bad as I'd feared.

He growled. "Which one? When you didn't answer, I started running that way, trying to get there as fast as I could. I just kept praying you wouldn't go inside alone. I didn't see any other wolves when I got there."

"I don't know. All I can tell you is that it was black, and much smaller than you. I hesitated at the wall, thinking I would wait for you, when I heard it growl behind me. I tried to talk to it but I couldn't, so then I tried to shoo it away, which also didn't work." I sucked in a breath at the memory. "About the time I decided the temple would be safer than trying not to get eaten, it sprang at me and grabbed my arm. I slammed my hand against it and hit it with my magic. I'm sorry, I injured one of your pack."

"What? Are you kidding me? Do not apologize. If it was one of my pack, they all were warned that you are under my protection. Harming you means their death.

How did you get away from it?"

"Once I smacked it, I was able to pull my arm from its grip and I fell over the wall. It knocked the wind out of me, but the second I was able to get up, I made a beeline for the temple. It was still whimpering on the ground when I got inside."

"Well, like I said, it was gone by the time I got there. But I will figure it out, and they will pay. All I had to do was cross the ruins and walk into the temple which was aglow with blue light. I could see it from outside. I just followed it until I found you."

"I'm sorry. But, how did you get in? Weren't there walls blocking the passage?"

"No. I just walked right down the hall."

He reached out and grabbed my hand, squeezing it. "What were you doing at the temple?? Why on Earth would you go there alone? She almost killed you." His voice trailed off at the last sentence.

"I don't know." I could barely whisper my response. I looked out the window, stalling. No cloud hung over the temple location.

He shook his head, and I just knew in his mind he lamented my stupidity. "If I had been five seconds later, you would be dead. As it was, I found you unresponsive, not breathing, and cold as ice. I thought for sure I had lost you." He inhaled with his eyes closed, taking a minute to steady himself. "Never, ever go there alone again. Why didn't you call me? I would have gone with you."

"I don't know." I repeated my answer from a moment ago, the only one I had to give him. "The evil spirit. She has the crescent mark, just like I do. It's even in the same place. And she looked oddly familiar, although I couldn't place where I might have seen her before." I licked my lips, trying to dispel the parched feeling. "She was so powerful."

Isaiah looked at me, taking in the information. His brows drew together. "You think you might know her from somewhere? She's been there for a long time."

With a shrug, I shook my head. "Maybe she just reminds me of someone. There is a book over on the dresser where my aunt had a list of others who bore the mark. It's got a green leather cover. Will you please bring it to me?"

He did as I asked, handing over the volume I requested. I flipped through the pages for a moment, looking for the chart I remembered reading about in one of my aunt's journal entries. I'd been meaning to look it over and hadn't had the chance.

Exactly in the middle, I found what I looked for. A family tree took up the majority of the spread, with coded lines leading to other witches outside our line who also carried the crescent birthmark. My own name had been the last to be added, with my mom and aunt above me. The line above the two of them carried a name circled in red.

Gretchen Reign. A line had been drawn through her first name. According to the chart, the woman was the mother of my mother and my Aunt Aimee. My grandmother? That couldn't be right. How had my own ancestor become so evil?

"I need to talk to my mom."

Throwing back the blankets, I swung my legs over the side of the bed, surprised by the sudden onset of acute vertigo. My head swam and stars danced before my eyes. Isaiah managed to catch me before I face-planted onto the hardwood floor.

"Maybe you should get back in bed and I should go and get your mom? You probably aren't ready to be up and about yet."

"How long have I been in bed?"

He hesitated. "Ah, about eighteen hours or so."

"What?!"

"Hey, that's not bad. It's better than being dead, right? And seeing how close you were to dying, I'd say a few more hours of rest shouldn't be out of the question."

The headache that throbbed through my skull didn't leave me any breath to argue with him. Easing my upper half back toward the pillow, I didn't protest when he lifted my legs back onto the bed, tucking the covers around me.

"Can you ask my mom to bring some Tylenol up with her when she comes, please?"

He nodded, slipping through the doorway and pulling it closed behind him. I took that opportunity to close my eyes and think about what happened in the room beneath the temple.

The scenes ran through my head over and over. I tried to slow them down to analyze every second of the encounter, but many of the details were still foggy. Unsure if it had something to do with the headache, or the magic, I gave up, waiting for the pain reliever that would hopefully help clear my head.

Isaiah returned, giving me a small smile. "Your mom said she will be right up. Do you want me to give the two of you a little privacy? I can go and come back later."

"Please stay. I think you need to hear this as well, and I have a feeling I am going to need a little moral support during the conversation."

Sliding the chair even closer to the bed, he took my hand. "I'm really glad I got to you in time. I don't know what I would have done if I would have been too late. Please don't ever do something like that by yourself again. Ever."

"I'm sorry. It never even occurred to me that things might take such a dangerous turn. I'm not sure what came over me."

A knock sounded on the door frame. My mom poked her head in. "I have some Tylenol for you." She walked over and dropped two little white pills in my hand, then passed me a glass of water and turned to go.

"Wait, Mom. We need to talk."

She glanced at me. "When you are feeling better, then we can talk. You need to rest." She continued toward the door as she spoke.

"No." My voice stopped her in her tracks, and she turned to face me once more. "We need to talk right now. You have put me off and lied to me long enough."

"Excuse me?"

My eyes met hers in a level stare. "No more. Your secret is out. I want to know about your mother. My grandmother. The one you always want to avoid speaking of, that you change the subject if she is mentioned. You had the opportunity to be honest with me when we were downstairs looking through all those pictures and I asked about her. Yet you chose to lie to me then too. Sit. Please."

Isaiah stood and offered her his chair, moving a few steps away to sit at my feet on the end of the bed. She hesitated. The clouds in her eyes telegraphed her discomfort.

"What do you want from me, Leah?" She sighed as she sank into the chair.

"The truth. I think you owe me that. All this time you have kept your secrets. If you had been honest with me from the beginning, maybe Aimee wouldn't be dead."

The pain that flitted across her face made me feel guilty, but I couldn't relent. She would be perfectly happy to keep her little secrets and take them to her own grave if I didn't insist.

"Leah..."

"No, Mom. That spirit almost killed me too, your only daughter. And you still don't want to give me the information that could save my life? Why? What is wrong with you?"

She sighed, and a tear slipped down her cheek. For a woman who had shown very little emotion my entire life, I'd seen a lot of her tears these past few days. "This is what I wanted to avoid from the very beginning. When I took you away from this place, my hope was that the world of witchcraft and magic would never touch you. I prayed to the Goddess every single day to protect you, to save you from the mess I had been born into. The day you spilled your blood onto this soil, I knew my prayers had been ignored."

I waited patiently for her to continue, knowing that the longer a secret has been kept, the harder it is to speak out loud. She had started talking, so I didn't think she would stop now.

"This sanctuary has been in existence for generations. At one time it was the home of both shifters and witches. Our family lived here for a long time, in peace with the packs. My mother, your grandmother, was a powerful witch and the leader of her coven. Even so, she didn't receive the mark until she was older, after Aimee and I came along. She wasn't born with it like you were."

She kept her eyes trained on her hands, folded in her lap, as she spoke. I could feel the shame and embarrassment rolling off of her in waves.

"Getting the mark changed her. She'd never been a very affectionate woman, but she grew power hungry. She cared about nothing more than becoming more powerful. In spite of the long-standing rule that outsiders were not allowed in the sanctuary, she began bringing in outsiders in exchange for favors. Outsiders that never should have known about the sanctuary in the first place."

I glanced at Isaiah, trying to gauge how much of this he might know. He kept his face blank and did not meet my eyes.

"Some of them began to practice black magic while they were here. It disrupted the natural magic of the land. She was so drunk with her own power at that point that nothing we said could dissuade her. Her coven grew tired of it. The ones she brought into the safety of the reserve began killing the shifters and witches to drain their power, and still my mother did nothing to stop it."

She looked up, meeting my eyes. I could tell she was

begging me to understand.

"I left. Aimee got married, which angered your grandmother because her new son-in-law was a wolf shifter, and part of the pack that had been trying to drive her out. When we came for the wedding, my own mother told me that you would grow up to be just like her, because of your mark."

The tears were falling freely now. She didn't bother to try and hide her distress. Deep hiccuping sobs wracked her small frame. Isaiah left the room briefly and returned with a handful of tissues.

"The coven finally had enough. They moved on, left the sanctuary. But they came back once more. The wolf packs and the witches banded together one last time to overthrow your grandmother. They bound her power and cursed her to remain here for eternity. Out of all the witches, only Aimee was allowed to remain because of her marriage to Rick. The wolves chased out the outsiders who hadn't already left. With your grandmother no longer having any power, or so they thought, they left her spirit to wander the sanctuary."

"I don't understand, if they bound her power, how did we end up where we are today? That makes no sense."

"I missed much of the goings on because I wanted no part of it for either of us. I siphoned off all my magic and stored it for safe keeping. I wanted you raised with no magical influence. As you know, Aimee and I were never in agreement about that. I believe she realized that your grandmother's powers had not been bound completely, or that she somehow managed to regain them. That is why she imprisoned her in the temple."

"You knew all about the magic in the world, and yet when I brought it up you tried convincing me that it wasn't real? You treated me like you thought I was losing my mind! You lied to my face over and over again!"

"Leah, please! I thought I was protecting you!"

"Protecting me? How? I almost died. And do you know, that when she was suffocating me, she told me that if either you or Aimee had trained me as I grew that I would be more powerful than she could ever hope to be and it would have been no contest between us? She said instead she would just drain all my power and use it for herself. Had you given me my birthright, Aimee wouldn't be dead either! Your selfish choices are what may have doomed us all!"

My mother covered her face with her hands and

cried. Her shoulders shook with the force of her grief. Isaiah stared at the floor, his discomfort obvious. I watched my mom cry, trying to temper the anger I felt with some sympathy. In my head, I tried to tell myself she had done what she thought was best at the time. Yet, I couldn't help but think that maybe she had just done what was easiest for her.

With a last sniffle, she stood up. Her red-rimmed and puffy eyes bored into mine. "You don't get to judge me, young lady. I'm sorry about what is happening now. I never wanted this. I tried to bind your magic as well, but even as a toddler you were too strong. All I could do was relieve some of it. I-"

"You tried to steal my magic?! Are you kidding me?" Her admission was the final straw. My anger bubbled up and over, out of control. "Get out! Get the hell out of here. I cannot believe you would ever do such a thing! If I fail, it will be entirely your fault!"

CHAPTER SIXTEEN

The door closed on my last words. Isaiah returned to the chair by my bedside. Rubbing my temples, I closed my eyes against the onslaught of pain, fear and frustration. My own mother had doomed me to failure.

"I don't think she did it to hurt you, Leah." His tone soothed my stress, even if it didn't help the real-life situation any.

"She lied to me my entire life. She continued to deny the existence of any type of magic, even when I showed her what I could do. And when I *suggested* there might be such a thing as wolf shifters, she acted like I had lost my mind. And she KNEW about them. She just kept pretending. It's one thing to not acknowledge magic when there is no evidence of it. But once we got here, and I actually started asking questions? She still lied to me. That's unforgivable."

"Give her some time. Now that everything is out in the open, she may be willing to give you more information. Just let her calm down for a while."

"I cannot believe that evil spirit is my grandmother. She gave birth to my own mother. It's a little embarrassing. What if everybody hates me when they find out?"

"Come on now. Everyone loved Aimee, right?"

"But I doubt anyone knew about the connection."

"Some of them might. Or at least they did once. You are doing everything you can to stop the evil spirit. Nobody will question your motives. That would just be crazy. She almost killed you for crying out loud!"

"Speaking of that, she also killed Aunt Aimee. She murdered her own daughter. Who does that?"

"We will defeat her. I promise. I'll be by your side every step of the way, and the pack will help in any way they can. Getting rid of her will be best for the sanctuary as a whole, and all of us living here."

"I appreciate your confidence, because I'm feeling like a failure right now. A total, miserable, failure. I waltzed right in there and almost let her kill me without even thinking about it."

Isaiah leaned over, bringing his face directly in line with mine. "You are not a failure. You made a mistake, and you're going to learn from it. She gave you some good information we can use against her. She said you are stronger than her. We just need to figure out how to use your power. She tried to kill you because she is afraid of you. We can use that."

"I need to know her name. The one in the book is not her real name, just the name she was known by. Even my aunt didn't seem to know her given name. I'll ask my mom, but she probably won't remember either."

"Let me go back to the pack and ask a few of the elders. Maybe they'll know. Someone, somewhere, must know her real name. I'll gather what information I can and be back later tonight. Just don't go anywhere alone, okay? Promise me, please."

"I won't leave the house, I promise."

He leaned in and kissed my forehead, barely brushing his lips against my skin. "Stay safe."

Without another glance at me, he got up and left the room. I heard his voice as he spoke to my mom on the way out, but couldn't understand the words. I didn't hear her response, either, if she made one. The back door clicked shut and silence settled over the house.

The need to get out of bed and keep working on finding a way to destroy the spirit – my own grandmother – washed over me. The need to rest wasn't nearly as important as ensuring she never managed to escape her prison. She would destroy me if she got another opportunity, and I couldn't let her get that chance.

A soft knock sounded at the door, followed by my mom poking her head in. "Can I come in?"

"Yes, please." I swung my legs over the side of the bed once more, determined to get up this time. "I'm sorry, Mom."

I needed to apologize to her, even though I fully believed that everything I had said was warranted. She deserved a little grace, too. Isaiah made a good point when he'd said that she hadn't done it to hurt me. If there was anything I truly believed in, it was my mother's love for me. She would never purposefully do something to endanger me.

She rushed over to sit in the chair Isaiah had vacated not long ago. "Sit. Wait. Please." She held her hands out to keep me seated on the edge of the mattress. "I'm sorry. You were right. About all of it. I let my fear guide my choices, and in doing so, made some decisions that were not in your best interest, even if I thought they were at the time."

My head shook from side to side as she spoke. "Let's just do what we can to fix it, okay? I'm going to need all the help I can get."

"Well, I don't know how much help I will be since I no longer have my magic. But I'll do what I can. Perhaps you can try a locator spell to find the missing pages? The ones that have the spell you need?"

"Why didn't I think of that? There were a couple written in the books that I read. I just glanced over them and never even gave them a second thought." I smacked my forehead with the palm of my hand in frustration, wincing at the stabbing pain that shot through my head in response. "Now, if I can only remember what book they were in..."

My mom grabbed my arm as I stood up, swaying a little with the dizziness. "Let me help you. Is it one of the books that is down here or do we need to go to the attic? I may not have any magic, but I do have a brain and I can make use of it."

"Maybe that brown one on the dresser? The thicker one, not the skinny one."

She handed me the book I had indicated, watching without speaking as I skimmed the pages. Unfortunately, my first guess had not been a good one, and the book didn't contain the locator spell I was looking for. My mom brought the entire stack to me and I flipped through each of them, page by page, finding nothing.

"I guess I was wrong. We'll need to go up to the attic."

"Let me go, I can bring down whichever ones you need."

I stood up, taking it slow to avoid any complications. "It will be easier if I go. I can recognize which books I have already looked through. It would be useless for you to just keep carrying books down that we may not need."

She slipped her arm through mine to help steady me. "Let's go, then. I'll help you navigate."

I winced at the pressure on my bitten arm, drawing her attention. She stopped, fixing me with her "mom" look.

"What is wrong with your arm?"

I gave her the abbreviated version of my encounter with the wolf. She shook her head, seemingly mystified.

"I can't believe one of them would attack you. In all the years our family has been here, there has never been an incident of one of us being attacked. Except your grandmother, of course, but that was warranted."

"I don't know that it was a shifter. It could have been a regular, wild animal. I tried to communicate with it but I couldn't get through."

"I wonder if she possessed it. Maybe she wanted to be sure you had no other options *but* to enter the temple where she could get her hands on you? And do you need me to take a look at it?"

That thought of possession had crossed my mind too, and I told her so. "I'm not going to worry about it anymore for now. The bleeding has stopped and we have bigger fish to fry. The bite wasn't as serious as I first thought. It should heal pretty easily."

"Okay then. Let's get looking for that book."

She moved to my other side and took my "good" arm. Together, we walked down the hall and made our way up the stairs. I had to take a breather before tackling the final staircase to the attic. Having the life almost sucked out of you really did a number on your body. By the time we got up to the attic, I had to sit down on the floor.

"We'll just go through them all up here and only bring the one we need back downstairs. That should give me enough time to get my breath back and hopefully you won't have to carry me back to bed!"

My mom chuckled, a sound I hadn't heard enough of lately. I looked up at her, pondering what she had been through. Not just these last few days, with the loss of her sister, but the majority of her life. Her childhood couldn't have been easy with a power hungry witch as her mother. Even after she escaped that situation, she ended up as a single mom, raising a baby witch who she never wanted to have any magic in the first place.

Her mother was bound and banished. Her brother-in-law disappeared without a trace. Then her sister was murdered by her own mother, who also tried to kill her daughter. I couldn't really blame her for not wanting much of anything to do with the magical community as a whole. I might have tried to get away from it too, had I been through all the things she had.

"Well, can you give us a little more light please?"

She shrugged her shoulders at my incredulous look. "At this point we need to use all the help we have available to us, and in order to read books we need to be able to see."

I spoke the single word, calling my own personal light bulb into existence with a grin. The thrill of doing any magic at all still felt very new to me, and I planned to enjoy it while it lasted.

"Did you know you can make it bigger, as well as brighter?"

My mom gave me instructions, teaching me how to adjust for the size and brightness I desired from the orb. For someone who hadn't used magic in a very long time, she still seemed to be familiar with it.

Of course, the spell we searched for ended up being in the second to last book in the pile, costing us a couple hours of time. We took it back downstairs, along with a few others my mom asked to bring, thinking we might be able to find something useful in them as well. We settled at the dining room table so I could read and practice while she made us something to eat.

"Food will help you get your strength back quicker. Your body needs fuel to recover. As you do more magic and begin working on bigger spells, you will find that your appetite increases exponentially. The more magic you do, the hungrier you will wind up being."

"Great. Just what I need."

My complaint was interrupted by a loud clap of thunder from the sky outside. Both of us jumped at the sound, which was strong enough to rattle the dishes in the cupboards. It sounded like it came from directly above the house. Peering out the window, I saw the little pair of chipmunks cowering on the window sill.

"Aw, the poor things. I'm going to let them in."

"What? They're wild animals, you can't just let them in the house! They'll poop everywhere and chew up the furniture!"

Ignoring her, I popped the back door open. "Come on in, you guys. Do you wanna come inside? It's a little scary out there, huh?"

They stared at me for a split second before taking me up on my offer and skittering between my legs into the dining room. My mom eyed them warily, but didn't make any more protests. Rummaging in the pantry, I grabbed a box of crackers.

"Are you hungry? Do you want a cracker?"

The two of them bounded up the dining room chair and onto the table, chittering loudly in response.

Curious if they would come closer, I held the cracker out in my hand, instead of putting it on the table for them to retrieve for themselves. After a very brief glance at each other, one of them crept forward, delicately taking the cracker from my outstretched fingers. He, or she, took it back to the other and then returned for a second one for itself.

My mom set a small bowl on the table. "Water. Crackers will make them thirsty."

A grin was my only response. She loved animals of all kinds just as much as I did. A sandwich and bowl of soup followed the bowl of water to the table.

"Eat, so we can do the spell."

I inhaled my lunch, eager to find out where the journal pages were hidden. Without them, there was no hope of reversing the curse on the wolf pack. Or making any other progress, really. My mom ran me through the process of performing the incantation and gave me some pointers.

I read through the words one last time and spoke them out loud. Nothing. All I could see in response to my request for information was inky blackness. Looking at my mom out of the corner of my eye, I tried a second time. Still nothing.

"There is something powerful blocking the spell. We may need to..."

Before we could say anything more, another clap of thunder exploded from overhead, and the lights went out. The chipmunks raced out of the room and disappeared. Hopefully, they didn't chew up the furniture like Mom had worried about.

"Damn it. The storm must have knocked out the power."

"Uh, Mom? Something tells me it wasn't the storm." Inky black vapor had begun creeping over the windows, looking for a way in. "I thought Aunt Aimee warded the house to keep the bad juju out?"

My mom jumped to her feet. "She probably did. The problem is that once she died, many of her spells began to lose their potency. The safety spells have slowly crumbled without her magic to shore them up. I didn't even think about that. We'll have to take care of it, but first we need to drive this stuff away."

An evil cackle filled the air. It brought me back to the moment in the temple when the spirit had begun to wrap her hex around me. I panicked. My mom, on the other hand, looked at me calmly. "You can take care of this. Follow my directions exactly."

She proceeded to give me step-by-step instructions. I mimicked her motions and repeated the words she said, matching her syllable for syllable.

"Et abierunt!" I thrust my hands, palms facing the doorway, toward the mist seeping through the seams of the glass.

An enraged shriek rent the air, but the encroaching witchery vanished. The moment my incantation was completed, the power flickered back on. I sank into the chair, sapped of energy. For a second, I was sure there wasn't enough food in all the world to replenish me.

"For someone who doesn't use her magic, you seem to still be pretty decent at it."

Mom sighed. "I've lost much of it. This was a simple spell, one of the ones that you practice on as you learn to harness your magic. It only stuck in my memories because of how many times I used it growing up. I used it to send away bugs, and snakes when out in the woods, and creepy strangers who approached me when I was out in public. It's a simple banishing spell."

"Does this mean that she has broken out of her cell?"

"No, but it means she is getting stronger, and the spell is getting weaker. She is able to send magic farther now, which means she will be able to reach you outside of the temple. We need to restore the wards on the house, and you will have to be extra vigilant from now on. We are running out of time."

CHAPTER SEVENTEEN

"She may have been the one blocking the locator spell. We need to assume at this point that she is strong enough to do just about anything. I want to try again with her gone and see if I can find the pages."

Mom nodded. "That's possible. She will do whatever she can to keep you from getting stronger. She knows if you can remove the curse on the wolves they will be firmly on your side and will do anything they can to help you rid the sanctuary of her altogether. She may be evil, but the one thing she isn't is stupid."

Before we can make another attempt, Isaiah jogs across the clearing and knocks on the back door. We motion him in.

"I felt the commotion and got here as quickly as I could. What happened?"

We filled him in, my mom explaining what we thought it meant for the spirit to be able to reach out to us from the temple. He frowned, replacing it just as quickly with a blank look, trying to hide his worry from us.

My mom reached out and touched his arm gently. "I am going to help Leah to shore up the defenses for the house. That will mean it can continue to be a safe space, while you prepare for the upcoming battle. After that, I have to return to our house to get something I think might help her. If you'd stay with her, I would appreciate it."

"What? You are leaving? And you didn't feel the need to tell me first?"

"It just occurred to me. I have some of your grandmother's things back at the house. They have been packed up and in the attic for years. It might point us to her given name, which will help give us the power to banish her when the time comes. I won't leave here until I know you will be safe though. The books will give us the information that we need to turn this house into a fortress. If I know Aimee as well as I think I do, there will be instructions down to the letter that she left for you, knowing that one day all of this would eventually be yours."

Isaiah agreed with her and looked me straight in the eyes. "As long as you are safe here, I think we need all the help we can get, and she should go get whatever she has that she thinks will be useful." He turned to my mom. "I will definitely stay here until you get back. We can find the journal pages and prepare for removing the curse."

"Let's get moving then. I am going to go into the library and find the book we need. Even after all these years, I think I have a good idea of what I'm looking for."

She left without waiting for either of us to respond. Isaiah pulled up a chair next to me, leaning his forearms on the table. I pulled the book with the locator spell over, positioning it between us.

"I already tried twice, but couldn't get anything. I think it was because the spirit was preventing me from accessing it. Now that she has been sent back to her bubble, I am going to try again. It *has* to work. It just has to. We need those pages."

Without waiting for his response, I closed my eyes, laying my hands over the pages of the book that contained the words. Nothing told me I had to do that, but it gave me more confidence to have a physical connection for some reason. I ran through the words once more in my head before saying them out loud.

A single image shimmered into view after I spoke the incantation. Despite focusing all my energy on the journal pages, the only image I got was of a tiny teacup. The white porcelain had dainty flowers painted all over it in hues of purple and pink. Gold edging ran around the rim. Not a single paper was in sight. In the bottom of the teacup, a single word had been penned. 'Revelare.'

"What the hell?"

Isaiah watched me patiently, not pushing me to tell him anything. My fingertips drummed a pattern on the wooden table top. The image turned over and over in my mind. Nothing I could think of would draw a connection between the missing journal pages and a tea cup. It didn't make any sense.

"I did something wrong. I must have." I replayed the entire thing for him, exasperation ringing in my voice.

"Maybe not. She wanted to be very sure that not just anyone could do the locator spell and find the pages. This is a clue for someone close to her, one only a few people might be able to figure out what the image means. Did she collect teacups?"

"Not that I know of. My mom might remember something that would help us, though. We can ask her when she gets back in here. I want to try again while we wait."

He didn't try to dissuade me, just sat next to me to lend me his support. Which I needed. Desperately. Failure wasn't an option, and yet I had no experience to bolster the natural power that everyone said I had within me. Everything I did, I did running blindly ahead, just hoping that I didn't find myself falling suddenly over the edge of a cliff to my death.

Repeating the spell got me the exact same image I had seen before, right down to the angle of the teacup as it hovered in my mind's eye. Either I was the suckiest witch to ever try witchcraft, or that teacup was what I needed to be looking for, whether it made any sense to me or not.

My mom returned to the room with a teal colored

notebook in her hands. "This is it. Everything you need to make sure that this house is impenetrable." She handed it to me.

Flipping open the cover, tears filled my eyes when I read the first page. Aunt Aimee had left me a note.

Dearest Leah,

I hope that you will never need to read these spells without me, that I will instead be here to teach you everything you need to know. But, just in case, I have written everything down for you. Each of these spells is meant to protect the house and the clearing, and by extension, you.

If you are, indeed, reading this without me, then the house is yours now. It holds many secrets, some of which will be easy for you to discover, and some that will not. The sanctuary itself holds a good many secrets as well, but those are for another time. If you are looking for ways to protect yourself, danger must have found its way to your door. It means that I have failed you, and for that I am so very sorry.

The grimoires contain just about everything you might need to know. Read them carefully. I will leave you other notes throughout them as well, if I get the chance. For now, follow these instructions. Do each page in the order it's written.

You have so much potential in you. The power you were

gifted will serve you well as you learn to master it. I have every faith that you will be amazing. If I never got to tell you this in life, I'm so very sorry. I wanted to every time we were together.

Love you always!

XOXO

Tears spilled down my cheeks, making reading her words almost impossible. I read them to myself three times before reading them out loud for my mom and Isaiah to hear. Thunder crackled again from the sky, interrupting the emotions I struggled to get under control.

"We need to do this right now." My mom looked out the window as she spoke. "There is no time to waste."

Flipping through the journal, I read each page quickly to give myself an idea of what I needed. Her instructions were detailed and thorough. They laid out where to stand, in what room and what direction I needed to face as I spoke the words. Some of them required me to touch certain objects. Others had me kneel on the floor, or put my hands on the wall. Each layer was meant to build on the ones before it, reminding me of the analogy of tying knots.

Isaiah and my mother followed me throughout the house as I performed each formula for protection. It took over an hour and drained me of what little energy I had left, but I completed the entire book. The storm raged outside as I worked, anger charging the air. The spirit knew what I was doing and was powerless to stop me.

My mom gathered her purse and keys, preparing to head to our house for the items she wanted to bring back to me. "Be safe, and please, stay in the house until I get back. Please."

"Don't worry, Mom. At this point, I know I need to rest and recuperate before I will be of any use to anyone. I'm about as strong as a newborn kitten right now." We walked her toward the front door. "I want to place a protection on you too. Just in case she tries to keep you from leaving."

I waited for her to make a protest, or flat out refuse. When she didn't I took it as acceptance. Laying my hand on her arm, I repeated the words I had found in the back of the notebook. She held still and didn't complain.

"I only need to make it off the sanctuary property. She cannot reach anything past the boundaries of this place for now."

Throwing my arms around her, I squeezed her tightly. "Please be careful. Oh! One more thing." I relayed what I had seen when I did the locator spell. "Do you have any idea what I should be looking for?"

"These spells are pretty straightforward. Look for the teacup. I'd be willing to bet it's around here somewhere, probably hiding in plain sight."

Isaiah and I stood on the porch and watched her as she maneuvered the car down the gravel drive and out of sight. Once her tail lights had disappeared from view, we latched the door and faced one another.

"Let's find that teacup, shall we?"

High and low we searched. In cupboards, on shelves and behind books. We opened boxes and lifted lids. Hours passed as we hunted for the elusive cup. The first go-round we did a visual check of every room. When we came up empty, we retraced our steps and did a more thorough search. Still nothing.

Starting in the basement, we methodically searched every nook and cranny. Not a hiding place went untouched. Every room in the house got the same treatment. By the time we made it into the attic, every single item in the building had been touched by one of us, most of them by both of us. While we found a few things that might prove helpful in the future, the location of the teacup itself remained a mystery.

I sank to the attic floor in defeat. My arm hurt, and the rest of my body wasn't in any better shape. My brain felt like mush. Frustration beat at me like an old lady trying to smack the dust out of a rug with a broom. And not the kind you could fly on, either.

Isaiah crouched down next to me. "Don't give up yet. We just need to get creative."

"Hmph. We've looked everywhere. I don't know that creativity is going to get us anywhere. I'm just so tired." So tired I wanted to cry, but even tears required energy I didn't have to spare.

He took my hands and gently pulled me to my feet, trying not to hurt me any more than I already was. The motion made me flinch anyway.

"Come on, let's go downstairs where you can rest in comfort while we come up with a Plan B."

"You might have to carry me," I replied, leaning into him for support just to remain standing.

"Can do." He reached for me to do just that.

"Ugh, stop. I'm just joking. I'll take all the support I can get down those stairs though."

Relying on him to keep me on my feet, we made it down to the living room where he maneuvered me onto the couch with a pillow behind my back and a blanket over my legs.

"Do you want anything? Need anything? Food? Water?"

"A quiet minute to think?" I teased him.

He grinned sheepishly and settled himself onto the other end of the couch at my feet. Quietly. Suddenly, a thought came to me.

"Oh man, I have an idea."

Flinging the blanket back, I hobbled to the center of the room, and spoke the word I saw written on the bottom of the teacup. Nothing. I moved from room to room, Isaiah following along behind me, speaking the word out loud in each one. Finally, in my aunt's office, we hit pay dirt.

As I repeated the word for the seventh time, a soft glow came from the top shelf of one of the bookcases. In place of the picture frame that had been standing there just seconds before was the dainty teacup, resting on its saucer.

Isaiah took it down, handing me the prize. As soon as my hands made contact with it, images flashed before my eyes. I knew exactly where I needed to look to find the missing journal pages.

"Follow me!"

Without waiting for his response, I rushed down the stairs into the basement. Excitement gave me a temporary burst of energy. Following the feelings that I had received in the office, I shoved aside boxes and crates, digging through a large pile in the corner. At the bottom, near the back, sat a dilapidated cardboard file box. Dragging it to the center of the room, I lifted the lid, making sure not to destroy it.

Moving aside some books stacked on the top, I rooted around until I found the one I had seen in my vision. I opened it to the back cover, looking for the tiny symbol among all the printing. When I found it, I slid my thumbnail between the parchment and the cardboard. As they separated, it became obvious the cover was not nearly as thick as it seemed. In a hollowed-out section lay the journal pages we'd been seeking.

Aimee's handwriting covered them, every word written out for me to use. At the end she had made a note. Only nature's chosen can use this spell to its full potential. One must bear the mark to unleash the power held in this incantation. Use it wisely.

CHAPTER EIGHTEEN

"We found it." My hands shook as I held the papers. "We found them, which means I can remove the curse and restore the pack to their former selves. They will no longer be stuck as wolves."

"And the evil spirit can be banished forever."

He swept me up in a hug and twirled me around the room. Unable to contain my laughter, and in spite of the pain, I threw my arms around his neck and looked into his eyes, which sparkled with mischief. All the aches and pains disappeared for a brief minute. Nothing felt better than success.

"Let's take this downstairs. I need to eat something and I want to start practicing. I think there are more paragraphs about reversing the curse in one of the books."

We entered the dining room to a disaster. The pair of seemingly harmless chipmunks had been chewing on the books we left sitting on the table. Shreds of paper, some over a century old, covered the tabletop and the floor. The little rodents stopped chewing at my outraged cry. Without giving it much thought, I clapped my hands together and spoke a single word.

The spell snatched the two little critters off the table and held them suspended in a bubble above the table top, their angry chatter filling the room.

"Why? Why would they do this?"

Isaiah slung his arm around my shoulder. "They're wild animals. I don't think they gave it any thought. Rodents chew. It's what they do."

"But... the books. And the spells. There was so much inside these books that I haven't committed to memory yet." Tears of frustration welled up.

Those tomes held the history I hadn't had the opportunity to learn in person. The only connection to my past and my magic lay within the ink on those pages. No other way for me to acquire that knowledge existed, and these two furry cretins had just destroyed a huge part of it.

Angry me wanted to squash them like tiny bugs and fling their carcasses out into the forest as a warning to any other nuisances that might be considering entering my space. Logical, slightly more humane me just wanted to send them far away so they couldn't ruin anything else while I wasn't looking. Even worse, I had nobody to blame but myself. I invited them in even when my mum warned against it.

Leaving the two in their respective bubbles for the time being, I chanted a spell to gather every last shred of the books and sealed them in a garbage bag. There must be a way for me to return them to their original state. Something like that had to be doable, with all that magic was capable of. Hopefully the little bastards hadn't actually ingested any of the pages. Even magic couldn't undo some things.

I sank into the wooden chair, propping my head in my hands. Isaiah moved through the kitchen, asking me what I wanted to eat.

"To be honest, I've lost most of my appetite at this

point."

"You have to eat. You are working your way up to doing some serious mojo and you need to fuel your body if you expect it to carry you through and help you to be successful."

Knowing he was right didn't help my mood any, and I scowled in his direction. To add insult to injury, my stomach chose that moment to growl, calling out my lie about losing my appetite. I slapped my palm on the tabletop.

"Fine. I'll eat. I'll eat whatever you make for me, just don't ask me to pick something."

He tried to cover his chuckle by banging the cupboard doors and pots and pans, but I heard him anyway. My eyes bored into his back, willing him to feel my glare. All I got in response was a view of his shaking shoulders as he tried his damnedest to not laugh out loud.

"Hmph."

I turned my attention to the journal pages we had finally found, reading through the words and notes scribbled on the pages. The complete incantation filled the first page, with notes about pronunciation scattered where my aunt had thought they might be needed.

Following the indications on the sheet, I practiced some of the more complicated words out loud, knowing I would need to recite them perfectly when the time came to actually go and remove the curse on the wolves.

The smell of frying bacon interrupted my thought process, enticing my stomach to growl again, more loudly than before.

"Only a few more minutes," Isaiah assured me as he grabbed plates and silverware.

He placed a cup of coffee in front of me, drawing my eyes to the unicorn mug. Memories of filling it with cocoa while Aimee had her coffee swamped me. Reaching out my finger, I gently traced the features painted on the ceramic. The scent rising from the mug reached my nose, smelling exactly how my aunt once took her own coffee. Tears fell from my eyes. Doubt swamped me.

She had been a witch her entire life and could not successfully contain the evil spirit. Who was I to think I might be able to do what she had failed at? Crescent mark or not, I had less than a week of magical experience under my belt, and every single thing I had learned came from my own studies. How did that stack up to an evil who had been practicing for years before my birth? An evil who also bore the crescent mark?

Isaiah's hand on my shoulder startled me. He set a plate in front of me, then pulled up the chair next to me.

"Don't cry, Leah. We'll manage. You can do this. I'll be by your side the entire way."

"But what if I can't? Aunt Aimee practiced for years and didn't make it. Who am I to think I might be successful where she failed?"

"You have to have faith. The mark will help you. Trust in it."

He said nothing more, picking up the fork and stabbing a piece of potato with it. He placed the fork in my hand, eyebrows questioning. I could see the query in his eyes. Was I going to eat the breakfast he made for me or let it go cold? Sighing, I took the bite, instantly glad I did.

"Mmm. This is *so* good." The potatoes had been perfectly seasoned and fried to perfection.

Satisfied, he turned his attention to his own meal, and we ate in silence, each of us lost in our own thoughts. Every last morsel he'd prepared got devoured. I even finished the bits left on his plate that he hadn't had the room to eat.

I practiced the spell for the rest of the day,

repeating the words until they were burned into memory. So much time was spent staring at the sheet of journal paper that the faded blue lines wavered in and out of focus, swimming beneath the writing.

Mid-afternoon brought another attempt by the spirit to infiltrate the house, though she was unsuccessful. Had it not been for the nervous chattering of the chipmunks in their temporary habitats, we may never have known about the incident.

Glancing at them with irritation, I demanded to know what they were going on about. "Maybe if you hadn't gnawed on my books, you wouldn't be in there!"

It wasn't until Isaiah followed their gaze out the back window that we noticed the black haze once more seeping from the forest. This time, however, it couldn't pass into the clearing, much less approach the house.

"Looks like the wards you put up are holding perfectly."

"That's a plus. I can concentrate on the spell without worrying about a sneak attack, now that we've seen for our own eyes that they are strong enough. For now."

By midnight I felt I had as good a handle on the spell as I was likely to get. Isaiah urged me to go lay down and get some sleep, reminding me my body needed to be in tip top shape for the next day.

"I'll be here all night. You have nothing to worry about except getting some rest."

"I wonder if my mom will be back before we go? Or if she's just run off and doesn't plan to return." The last words tasted bitter on my tongue.

"She wouldn't abandon you now. She already feels guilty for her part in this. I could smell it on her when you two were talking. She feels responsible and I think she will do her best to help you in whatever way she can."

"Not that that will amount to much. She gave up her magic."

"She stored her magic," Isaiah countered. "That doesn't mean it's gone. She just needs to retrieve it and accept it once more. You're her only daughter, I think she would do that for you, if meant helping you succeed, and live."

His last word jarred my thoughts. Live. A chance remained that I, too, could die by going up against the evil spirit. My grandmother wanted me dead. She'd killed her own daughter with no remorse, and no hesitation. I had no doubt that if she could get me out of her way, she would remove me as well.

I shrugged and nodded my agreement. Too tired to continue arguing the situation, I slipped into the bathroom to get ready for bed. As I washed my face and brushed my teeth, I studied myself in the mirror. The brown eyes staring back at me looked the same as they had just a few days prior, before my entire world had been turned upside down. The WTF lines between my brows, however, had deepened considerably.

With a sigh, I promised myself some pampering when this whole debacle ended. Maybe there was a spell that could reverse the ravages of stress?

Slipping out of the bathroom in my pajamas, I returned to the kitchen to check on Isaiah, who held the two little chipmunks in their bubble. Oops. I'd forgotten about them. Since my anger had subsided, I felt bad about leaving them trapped in there for hours. They began chattering angrily at the sight of me.

"I'm sorry guys, I was mad. Those books were important. Not that I can use that as an excuse. Want a snack before I put you back outside?"

As a response, both of them turned away, leaving me staring at their furry little butts. Sighing, I grabbed a couple of cookies and opened the back door. I put the cookies on the table they always got their crackers on.

"See? They'll be here if you change your mind. I'm sorry, I really am."

Neither of them deigned to give me a response, and I sighed. Sending the bubble out into the middle of the clearing, I rested it on the ground and released them. They took off like a shot, scampering for the nearest tree. One of them turned back, waving his little front paws and chattering loudly at me, before racing up the tree to join his friend.

I turned to Isaiah and lifted my hands, palms to the sky. "Apparently mending fences is not my forte."

He latched the back door behind me, throwing the deadbolt. "They'll come around. Cookies are hard to resist. Now go get some sleep."

"What about you?"

"I'm going to keep my eyes on a few things and reach out to the pack. I'll nap on the couch when I'm ready."

The linen closet held spare blankets and pillows; the entire time I spent grabbing bedding for him, I toyed with the idea of inviting him to join me in my room. It held a king sized bed and would give us each plenty of room. Unable to bring myself to voice the question out loud, I just handed him the stack and smiled.

"You know where to find me if you need me."

"And I'll be right out here if *you* need anything. Just yell and I'll come running."

As I walked down the hall, I mentally kicked myself for not at least asking him if he wanted to sleep in the room my mom had been using. Instead of turning back, though, I left my door open a crack and slipped beneath the blankets.

In spite of the nerves stretched to the breaking point, I managed to fall into a deep sleep. Not a single thought or dream invaded my rest, as if my mind knew that I needed every bit of an advantage I could get for the next day, and it shut everything off at the source.

Six am came early, but I woke feeling energized and refreshed. As I dressed for the day, I went over my plan. At the first light of day we would head out for the stream and the first step of banishing the evil spirit from the sanctuary forever. I would reverse the curse and free the wolf pack from her spell that had been plaguing them for years. They would once more be able to shift with ease and access their memories. If I could pull it off.

Which was a pretty big if. Did I have the power to

perform such a huge undertaking? All I could do was pray I did. I'd give it everything I had in me, and hopefully that would be enough. It had to be.

Isaiah sat at the kitchen table, a mug of steaming coffee in front of him. He smiled when I walked in and got up to pour me a cup too.

"Ready?"

Accepting the mug, I gave him what I hoped was an encouraging smile. "As ready as I'll ever be."

He had a lot riding on my success, too, and I worried what would happen if I failed him. As the alpha, he held all the responsibilities to the pack for making them whole once more. A task that was far beyond his capabilities. Which meant he needed me to help him. My fear was that the help he needed fell beyond my capabilities as well.

We ate a quick breakfast and finished clean up by the time the first streaks of light shot across the sky. My backpack had been filled with anything and everything I thought I might need the night before. I heard a few wolves howling in the distance.

"Do they know?"

He nodded. "I spoke with my new beta, Sam, last night. I can trust him. They will accompany us, at a distance, in case we are in any need of back up."

Our hiking boots made soft footfalls on the pine needle covered path. The earthy smells rising from the loamy ground tickled my nose. At one point Isaiah reached out and grabbed my hand, giving it a quick squeeze before dropping it again. Our gazes bounced off each other before returning to the trail in front of us.

The trek to the stream both took more time than expected and yet seemed to be over in an instant. Walking right up to the shoreline, I stopped cold. Somehow the evil spirit had gained an advantage, making her first move before we arrived.

The stream bed lay in front of me, dry as a bone.

CHAPTER NINETEEN

How on Earth was I supposed to remove the spell from a stream that no longer existed? My eyes met Isaiah's, stunned. Defeat rolled through my body, my shoulders sagging towards the rocky stream bed. My chin felt like it weighed a thousand pounds. My nails dug into my palm, no doubt leaving tiny crescent shaped indentions.

"What the hell?!" I screamed my frustration into the air.

Isaiah grabbed my arm gently. "Hey. It's okay. We'll figure it out."

"How, pray tell, will we figure it out? I've only got so much magic and so much ability." I yanked my arm from his grasp and turned so my back faced him. "And so much time. I'm not cut out for this."

As I studied the ground at my feet, mournful howls filled the air. They somehow knew that we had reached an obstacle we might not be able to overcome. My feeling of responsibility to them also reminded me that it wasn't about me. Their sorrow drove me to pull up my big girl panties and find my way out of my pity party.

I turned back to him once more. "Okay. I need to think. Maybe, if I draw in enough power, I can reverse the curse anyway. I have to at least try."

Isaiah gave my arm an encouraging squeeze, but didn't say a word. He didn't have to. I saw in his eyes the faith he had in me. His belief in me is what drove me to want to be better, try harder, go further.

The second I began to pull on the latent power surrounding me, my vision dimmed and I found myself once more in the land of the wispy white mist. Unsure, at first, of whether I'd been transported to the safe, peaceful place or the place of frozen fear, I waited with bated breath. As a swath of mist wafted towards me, I reached out my hand and ran my fingers through it. A sigh of relief escaped when there was no biting cold to meet them.

"Leah..."

The voice from my first trip to this land of peace floated from the edges of my consciousness. Searching for the source of the words, I spun in a circle but saw nobody. I heard no footsteps or other sounds of anyone else being present.

"Leah." This time the voice came from directly behind me.

As I turned, my aunt's form took shape in front of me, dropping me to my knees. "Aunt Aimee."

The tears spilled over, and nothing could have stopped them from falling at that moment. To look upon her once again, even in this spectral form, drew emotion deeper than I could hope to control. The circumstances of the last few days haunted me. The guilt I felt for not coming to see her, and the sorrow of knowing that I never would again.

"Don't cry, child. There is no time for tears."

"But, I miss you. I need you. I can't do this without you. Why didn't you ever tell me about all this? I feel like I am stuck trying to win a race that I didn't even know I had entered until all the other contestants were almost at the finish line!"

Her face remained stoic, no emotion showing. She inclined her head slightly, but gave no other indication that she had heard my pleas. When she began to speak again, it was not to answer my questions or allay my fears.

"Hidden here near the stream bed is a talisman. You must find it. It will aid you in your quest to reverse the curse. The dry steam bed is only an illusion. Reach out with your sight and you will be able to perform the spell."

Her spirit floated over the ground, leading me to a gnarled tree trunk, long dead. Ivy in the deepest brown covered the majority of the stump. The color indicated it had long given up its hold on life, and yet it did not crumble at my touch. Shoving it to the side unearthed a small hollow within the wood.

At my aunt's encouragement, I reached in, feeling around blindly. My fingers brushed cold, cylindrical-shaped metal. Plucking it from its hiding place, I drew out a silver talisman on a heavy chain. Wrapping my hand around it, I turned to face her once more.

Instead, an empty clearing greeted me. She no longer stood at my back. "Aunt Aimee? Where are you?

Please don't go yet. I need you!"

The tears continued to fall, but her image never returned to the glade. Pain tore through me, leaving my eyes squeezed shut and my jaw clenched. From a distance I heard someone calling my name, but couldn't bring myself to answer. As the voice got closer, it became more insistent.

"Leah. Leah. Are you all right?"

Slow blinks brought Isaiah's face into focus. For the first moment, all I could do was shake my head. My knuckled ached from holding my hands so tightly that blood leaked from the small cuts made by my fingernails. The ringing in my ears competed with his voice.

"Where did you go? One second you were talking, and then all of a sudden you were gone. Your body was here, but I could tell that you had left me. Nothing I said or did could get your attention. You scared the shit out of me."

"I need to do the spell."

With a struggle, and Isaiah's hands guiding me, I staggered to my feet and ignored his queries. Following the instructions, I'd read to the letter, I began to perform the incantation. To help power the magic, I drew power in from the forest around me as I spoke the words I worked so hard to perfect.

My voice grew hoarse, and tears continued to make tracks down my dirty cheeks. Wind began to howl through the trees. Clenching the talisman, I continued to repeat the lines of the ancient language, even as I felt the blood begin to leak from my nose and run a sticky trail onto my upper lip. Isaiah had backed away, leaving me no support when my knees gave out and slammed into the rocky ground.

Resting on all fours, I let the power of the sanctuary flow through me, drawing it in just to force it back out with each syllable I uttered. Only dying would stop me from removing the curse on this stream and the pack of wolves that gathered around me.

The exertion left me with chattering teeth, impeding my ability to make complete phrases, but I kept forcing the sounds through my bloody lips as I chanted them in my head. My skin felt like it had a million fire ants biting into it. Wolves began to howl all around me, joining their voices with the wind.

Just when I thought I had failed, that my magic wasn't strong enough, that I had let them all down, the wind abated. Silence stole through the creek bed. At the same time my arms gave out, I vomited blood, splashing the crimson over the pale pebbles in front of me. Then it was face first into the ground and lights out for me.

"Leah. Can you hear me?"

A low groan took the place of the response I'd meant to utter. The words were not working quite yet. Attempting a nod brought on sharp pain, stabbing through my frontal lobe, and I quickly cut that off as well.

"Uh-huh." A whisper was all I could manage.

"Oh, thank the goddess. Don't you dare die on me."

"Not. Dead," I croaked.

His face swam into focus, his eyes replacing the stars that had been dancing across my vision. So far I could ascertain two things, that I remained in the land of the living, and I hadn't killed him either. Two tallies in the plus column.

Feeling weak as a wet dishrag, I made no rush to get up, in spite of the fact that the uneven ground below me killed my backside. It took a conscious effort to release the strain on my hands, loosening my grip. As I did, the talisman slipped from my fingers.

Isaiah batted it out of reach in alarm. "Where did you get that?"

Surprised as his reaction, it took a second for me to answer. "When I kind of got lost on you the first time, I ended up back at the glade I told you about. The one with the white mist everywhere? I saw my aunt. She guided me to the hiding place of the talisman. She told me it would help me to power the spell and reverse the curse."

"No. No, no..." He shook his head as he spoke. "She lied to you. That talisman is the one the pack used to break the evil spirits' connection with the sanctuary and begin the removal of her mark so that they could overpower her."

"What?" Shock echoed through me. "You must be mistaken. Why would she do that to me? She must know that I need my mark to perform the final spell to banish the spirit forever. I don't understand."

Turning my left palm upward and wiping away the blood and dirt, it became obvious that what Isaiah had told me was true. The color of the birthmark beneath the scar tissue was fading away. Even the scar tissue itself had begun to sink back into the skin, becoming smooth once more.

"We can get it back. You can heal yourself, but you will have to activate your wolf genes to do it."

"Wolf genes? What are you talking about?"

"The mark is only granted by the goddess to a very special person. That person must have both witch and werewolf genes. Such a hybrid is incredibly rare, because usually a werewolf can only mate with its own species, and if a pregnancy does result it is almost never carried to term."

"Are you telling me my father was a werewolf?"

"It explains why you were able to talk with me in wolf form, while others, like your mother, was not. Although just the fact that you have the mark tells me that, because there has never been a person to receive the mark who wasn't that particular lineage."

"I guess that is something we will have to ask my mother about when she returns. She never spoke of my father, not once. Eventually I quit asking because it was obvious that it upset her greatly when I wanted to talk about it. I have no idea if he is alive or dead even."

"Even if she won't tell you, we may be able to find out. The elders have kept genealogy records for many generations. If she didn't keep your birth a secret from your father, it may have been recorded somewhere."

"Wait just a minute. How do you know all of this all of a sudden?" It dawned on me that he was giving me information he'd been unable to provide every other time we had talked about my situation.

He paused. "My memories are clear. I can remember everything. You did it. The curse has been removed. Leah, you did it!"

His excitement was contagious, in spite of how terrible I felt at that moment. Knowing that my sacrifice hadn't been in vain, and I had returned the shifters to their true forms, restoring their abilities. And I had learned something about myself already, even if it meant that I had to accept the probability that my father had known he had a daughter and yet never once showed any interest in getting to know me. That cut deep. Of course, I had known that to be a possibility to begin with. Perhaps he had been the one to leave us, and not the other way around.

"I didn't actually need the talisman to perform the spell, did I?" Sadness almost smothered me, knowing I had severed my connection to nature, and possibly lost my ability to do magic forever.

"No. You had more than enough power to perform it on your own. But we'll get your magic back. And your mark fades slowly. We need to banish the spirit before it is erased completely. We also need to put this thing somewhere safe, where something like this won't happen again."

"I can't believe she betrayed me." My heart shattered at the thought that she would deliberately sabotage my effort to complete the very thing she had been working toward. The cause she had died for.

"Are you sure it was actually her?"

His question brought more confusion than clarity. "What? It certainly looked and sounded just like her. Although, she didn't seem to have any emotion at all. Even as I cried and begged for her help, she just kept directing me to where the talisman was hidden, saying I needed it to remove the curse."

"The evil spirit is powerful. Perhaps she pretended to be your aunt to trick you into touching the talisman. She knew you would trust your aunt's image before you would ever listen to a stranger."

"That bitch." Now I was pissed off. How dare she?

"If she did, it means that her powers are growing, and we need to end her quickly. If she breaks that containment spell and regains her full strength, we will have an even bigger fight on our hands. We need to get moving, but you need to rest. There is no way you can go up against her in this state."

"I can do it. We need to go." I struggled to stand.

"You've lost a lot of blood and you need to eat and rest, at least for a couple of hours. Let's get you back to the house and replenished. Then we will go, I promise. We need to check in with the others as well and make sure the removal of their curse didn't do any damage."

"Two hours. Then we are getting rid of her once and for all."

He grinned down at me. "Yes, ma'am."

CHAPTER TWENTY

Since I refused to sleep, Isaiah took on the job of feeding me while I reviewed the spell to finally banish the evil spirit for good while I "rested" at the dining room table. A veritable buffet of smells wafted from the stove as he cooked, interrupting my ability to concentrate.

With a flourish he set a steaming plate in front of me, piled high with eggs, bacon, sausage and hash browns. To the side of that lay a saucer with English muffins slathered in butter. He refilled my coffee mug, adding a perfect mixture of cream and sugar.

Ensconced in the chair next to me, he brought himself a plate with much smaller portions on it. A single glance at it and I raised my eyebrows.

"Wow. Way to make a girl feel self-conscious about how much she eats," I teased him between bites. Not that it would stop me from devouring every last morsel on my plate. My appetite demanded to be appeased in a way that brooked zero arguments.

He laughed. "Hey. After shifting, I eat like a starving bear too. Magic drains a lot from the human body, and that's nothing to be ashamed of." He followed his verbal reassurance with a wink. "And it's not like you have anything to worry about, anyway."

A blush stole up my cheeks. Warmth that had zero to do with my hot breakfast or scalding coffee curled in my midsection.

A faint itch nagged at my palm. The crescent mark was nothing more than a pale representation of what it had once been. My ability to do the powerful magic was fading faster than we realized. If I didn't get to the temple before the dark spirit broke free, she would have free rein throughout the sanctuary, and we would be helpless to stop her.

"We need to go. I don't know how much time I have

left before the mark disappears completely."

He glanced at my half eaten breakfast, then up at my face. "Already?"

I held out my hand to show him the mark. "It's itching faintly, which means there is growing magic around, but it's fading so fast. We don't have the time to dilly dally. Whether I am ready or not, we have to go. We can rest later, if we live through this."

He grabbed my outstretched hand. "Don't say that. We will live through it."

Standing, he pulled me up with him. "I've asked the pack to surround the temple and stay nearby. As alpha, I can pull power from them to bolster me, which I can then share with you if needed. It's the best I can offer you as assistance."

My fingers curled around his. "Thank you." My words were soft.

Without another word, we exited through the back door. Dishes were left on the table, evidence of our hastily eaten breakfast. Half-empty, the coffeepot sat on a trivet between the two place mats. Thoughts flitted in and out of my head. Would I ever see that kitchen again? In my heart, I knew that the likelihood of me failing, and possibly dying, today wasn't necessarily small. We hadn't even heard from my mother since she left. At least if I died, I'd be with Aunt Aimee.

Dark gray thunderclouds covered the sky above, blocking out the sun. They danced and swirled on the unnatural wind, churning and frothing like ocean waves. An eerie silence filled the air. No birds squawked, and the ever present chipmunks made nary a chatter, although I could attribute their absence to our earlier incident. Even the wind blowing through the trees made almost no sound.

Walking the path to the temple took longer than expected, thanks to the resistance the dark spirit had sent out. Instead of an easy walk up the clear trail, my legs fought for every inch forward like I tried to wade through thigh high wet cement. Even Isaiah struggled. But we never stopped.

As we drew closer, we were able to spot some of the pack members as they paced nervously. Sam, Isaiah's new beta, met us at the entrance to the ruins in his wolf form.

"Are you guys sure about this?"

I snorted, a very unladylike noise. "No. But at this point there are no other options. I am simply going to do my best. Pray to your goddess, or whoever else you look to for guidance, because I am going to need all the help I can get." A clap of thunder punctuated my sentence.

Isaiah sent out a final message to the pack, knowing that once we got inside there would likely be no way for us to communicate. Hands clasped, we stepped over the crumbling wall and into the temple yard. A feeling of sorrow and dread swamped us both like a rogue wave. It took an immense effort to move forward, shuffling instead of walking because I could barely lift my feet off the ground.

Before stepping through the doorway, I took one last inhale of fresh air into my lungs. The air inside was sure to be heavy and dense, just like before. As we entered the doorway, the inner sanctum was bathed in blue light. It pulsed into the room from the hallway that led down to the room where the spirit fought to break out of her prison.

"She must be close to breaking free of the spell. We need to hurry."

I crossed the room to the destroyed alter. Common sense told me that if my aunt had been paying homage to it, and the evil spirit had chosen to destroy it, whoever the alter was meant to honor must be on my side. It couldn't hurt to spend a few seconds asking for their help.

Kneeling on the step, I righted the heavy metal bowl that had once sat front and center. From my pocket, I took the key that had once opened the door to the cell below. That door no longer existed, so I couldn't see needing to keep it. Crafted from magic, it represented a part of this temple that I now returned to whomever created it.

"I have very little to offer you at this moment, but I come humbly asking for your help. This evil cannot be allowed out into the world. Please, if you have any way of aiding me to defeat her, I ask that you do so." My voice could barely be classified as a whisper, but I knew the deity would hear me if he or she was there to listen. Whether or not I would receive their assistance was another matter entirely.

Isaiah helped me to my feet, and we walked silently toward the hall that led down into the earth. Instead of the long, spiral walkway I followed on my last trip, this journey took only seconds. We rounded a second curve and came face to face with the spirit, standing in her human form, pressing against the boundary that kept her ensnared.

"I knew you would come, and you brought your little puppy along as well. But you're too late, and too weak to stop me now."

Her cackle grated on my ears, making me wince. Isaiah stood solidly next to me, not even gratifying her with a response. He put gentle pressure on my fingers, subtly reminding me of his support. It bolstered my confidence.

"You will not be free."

"This spell has been crumbling and weakening since Aimee drew her last breath right above me. At this point, there is nothing you can do to keep me here. Not without your connection to the sanctuary to give you power."

"You pretended to be Aimee just to trick me. You're a monster. You killed your own daughter."

"And as soon as this final remnant of the dungeon breaks, I will kill you too. I will drink down your power for my own and leave you nothing more than a lifeless husk on this dirty floor."

The venom in her voice pierced me. The figure before me was of my own family, had been my flesh and blood. And to her, I was nothing.

The words of the incantation began falling from lips

without conscious thought. The blue light dimmed as the spirit laughed. Still, I continued.

As I spoke, the floor began to tremble. Dust and pebbles began to rain down from the ceiling. It seemed like only seconds before I felt the first trickle of blood drip from my nose. My eyes remained trained on the blue bubble in front of me. Using my hands, I mimed as if making a snowball compressing it tightly. A shriek rent the air as I managed to force her from her human form back into the misty vapor encapsulated by the orb.

My entire body began to tremble as I used up every ounce of force I possessed. Isaiah took that to be his cue and began feeding me his own strength. It worked, temporarily. It gave power back to my voice, and I continued reciting the words I'd memorized from the journal page. Over and I over I fed them with my magic, forcing the orb to grow smaller and smaller.

I registered the difference in energy when Isaiah exhausted his own and began drawing from the pack. In order to conserve every last ounce of my strength, I sank to the floor, kneeling and motioning Isaiah down with me. Tears poured down my cheeks from the effort. Sweat gathered on my forehead, running down and mixing with the tears. Wiping them away, my hand came back crimson, covered not in salty clear liquid, but more blood.

My arms ached, as if the weight of the world rested on them while I tried to force the small orb to shrink away into nothing, taking the spirit with it.

Isaiah's body brushed against me as he fell, face first, onto the floor and out cold. My concentration broke as I screamed his name, giving the spirit an opportunity she wasted no time in taking. Cracks appeared in the orb, allowing the inky black mist to swirl through them.

Her voice echoed through the chamber. "It's over, little one. You have lost."

Screaming with the effort, I regained my focus. "No!"

I began the chant again, giving it everything I had. At that moment I knew I fought for my life, and the life of every inhabitant of the sanctuary. If she escaped, she would drain them all dry. In a battle of words versus wisps, the black vapor fought to reach me. If it did, I would be done for.

My voice faltered, lowering to a whisper, but still I continued. Every bone in my body ached and cried out for respite. Blood dripped down onto the cellar floor, settling on the surface of the packed dust. As I focused on the droplets, a searing headache brought stars into my vision, and still I murmured the spell. But the evil vapor grew even closer.

The moment it reached me, its icy fingers trailed over my cheekbones, causing me to shiver so hard my teeth clattered against themselves, interrupting the flow of words. Taking a deep breath in an attempt to begin again, I choked as the haze wound its way through my lips and down into my lungs, forcing out the much needed oxygen. It wrapped around my throat and crawled into my nose, blocking my only other way to get a breath.

A sharp pain stabbed my palm, and a final look showed that the crescent mark had disappeared from sight, no longer marring the skin where it had existed my entire life. Another tear fell, this one at the loss of a piece of my identity. My vision narrowed as the lack of life-giving air began to shut down my systems.

In the last seconds, the spirit retook her human form, striding from the center of the room to stand before me.

"I told you that you weren't strong enough to defeat me. Now look at you. Seconds left in this life and your final sight will be of me, right before I waltz out this door and back into the world you tried so pitifully to protect."

Rapidly blinking in an attempt to clear my vision, the next thing I saw was a flash of white hot light. A scream echoed in my ears as the smoky substance retreated from my lungs, giving me the ability to breathe for the first time in what felt like very long minutes.

The blue light shot out the doorway and disappeared. After that, there was nothing but blackness.

"Leah. Leah, honey, can you hear me?"

Warm hands pressed against my shoulders, shaking me gently, as a voice filtered into my consciousness. As much as I wanted to open my eyes, the lids felt like they were cemented shut. Pain raked through my body like bolts of lightning. With great effort I managed to roll onto my side before every last morsel of the breakfast Isaiah had cooked for me fled my stomach.

"Isaiah!"

What I'd intended to be very loud came out as a whisper, but fear forced my eyes open as I looked for him. My struggle to sit up proved useless against the hands holding me down.

"Shh... he will be okay, please rest for just a minute."

Recognition dawned as I drug my eyes from Isaiah's prone form to the face above me. "Mom?"

Tears streamed down her face. "Baby, I'm so sorry. I got here as quickly as I could."

"You? You defeated her? What happened to having no magic?" Anger spilled over into my voice.

"Please listen. I returned to the place I had hidden my magic so that I could take it back, so that I could help you. It proved to be more of a struggle than I had anticipated. And no, I didn't defeat her. I stopped her from killing you, but she escaped."

Escaped. The word was bitter to my ears. Everything I had just endured was all for nothing.

"So I failed."

My mom shook her head. "No. Not completely. I couldn't keep her from breaking the binding to the temple, but she is tied to the sanctuary, she cannot leave this chunk of land. We still have a chance to prevent her from having free rein of the world."

"We? Excuse me?"

"I've regained my magic and accepted my place in

this world. I will teach you anything you want to know. Everything I've ever learned."

"Are you kidding me? Now? Now you all of a sudden want to help me? When you spent my entire life hindering me? If it wasn't for you trying to keep me from learning about magic in the first place, this never would have happened. I would have been strong enough to defeat her, she said so herself."

"I'm sorry. I was wrong, and I know that now. I want to help you. Please."

"GET. OUT." Anger gave my voice strength as I screamed the words at her. "I don't even want to look at you. This. Is. *Your.* Fault."

She gasped, the hurt evident on her face. She reached out and touched my hand. I felt the power crossing from her to me. "At least let me heal you."

I snatched my hand from her reach. "Get. Out. I don't need your help."

She paused, then pivoted away from me, tears running down her face. Stopping for a moment, she reached down and touched Isaiah's shoulder. In spite of wanting to yell at her not to touch him, I knew he needed her help. I couldn't heal him, so if she was willing to do so, I would let her. But that would be the last thing.

His chest lifted as air filled his lungs once more, and I crawled to him, paying her no mind as she backed away from us. I didn't see or hear her leave the room, as I focused entirely on Isaiah. His beautiful eyes opened, looking up at me.

"Oh thank the goddess." I laughed through the pain, thrilled to see him conscious. I hadn't gotten him killed after all.

"What happened? You did it? She's gone?"

I laid my hand on his chest, full of sorrow. "Not exactly..."

CHAPTER TWENTY-ONE

He sat up with a struggle, looking me in the eye. "What do you mean, not exactly? And are you okay? You look like death warmed over."

The breath that had been hanging out in my lungs rushed out my nose as I pressed my lips together in a frown. They separated with a pop thanks to the stickiness of drying blood when I opened my mouth to answer him. The words were slow to come, my shame at having failed him causing me to stutter.

"I'm sorry. I'm so sorry." Tears, actual tears,

streamed down my face. They mingled with the brick red smears on my cheeks and dripped off my chin tinged pink.

"Why? What do you have to be sorry for?"

He sat up, wincing slightly but otherwise seeming to be okay. My mother must have healed most of his injuries within that short time span she had her hand on him. She must have some very potent magic for it to be that easy for her. Magic that could have helped me over the years. Memories floated through my head of all the times I had been injured, or sick, that she just watched me suffer, when she could have fixed it in three seconds or less. It made me sick to my stomach. Even the injuries I'd received in the last few days had garnered nothing but pain reliever and band-aids from her.

Chasing all the thoughts of her from my head, I focused on Isaiah's face, ignoring his questions about myself for the moment. "Are you really okay? You're not in pain?"

He shook his head. "Nah. A little sore, and very tired, but otherwise fine. What happened? I don't remember much past kneeling down next to you."

I filled him in on the abbreviated version, faltering when it came time to tell him that my mom had saved my butt, but we let the spirit escape. Guilt ate at me. Even though I didn't want to, I managed to force the words from my lips, relaying the moment when I had thought my time was over. Until she entered the room with a blast of her magic.

"Leah. It's not your fault. Where did your mom go? I'd like to thank her for saving you, and the rest of us."

"What? Thank her? Did you hear anything I said?"

"I get that you're angry, but without her we all would have died. And we know the spirit remains tied to the sanctuary. The spirit did not win. You weakened her considerably. For now, she will have to go underground to hide and try to rebuild her powers. While she does that, we will get ready."

I decided to avoid talking about my mother for the time being, if I could. "How do I prepare?" I thrust my palm toward him. "I've lost it completely. My mark is gone and I doubt I will be able to do a lick of magic."

"That's not how it works. The magic is in you. You can heal your ability to create it. The mark simply enhanced your natural powers. I have to believe there is a way for us to try and get it back. There must be."

"I don't know how we're supposed to heal it."

Frustration ate at me, almost as painful as my

actual physical injuries. Temptation was equal between curling up in a little ball and sobbing my heart out and breaking everything in sight. Not that there seemed to be much left in the temple that hadn't already been broken by our confrontation.

"Remember, you're half wolf. We have incredible healing abilities. When we shift, we can heal most wounds that would be fatal to a normal human. We just need to get your wolf genes activated. Up and running, so to speak. If that doesn't work, we will find another way. Come here."

"But I don't know how to be a wolf! I've only known I was a witch for a few days and am far from mastering that half of my DNA. I'm not sure I have it in me to start over again to try and learn the ways of a wolf."

"But this time you have me. I'm a master at being a wolf, and I'll teach you everything you could possibly want to know. Probably more."

He reached over and pulled me into his lap, stopping as I cringed at the pain. He looked down at me sternly.

"Why aren't you healed? You said she healed me. Why didn't she heal you too?" Anger flashed in his eyes.

My gaze shifted away from him. "I wouldn't let her.

I was angry, and I screamed at her to get out. I only let her heal you because I knew I couldn't do it, and the thought of you suffering just because I didn't want her touching me almost killed me. There was no way I was going to chance losing you. I didn't know how badly you were hurt."

"Leah. You idiot," he chided me gently. "You need to heal. You should have let her help you. Even with her removing the physical injuries, you still would have had a long way to go before your body managed to deal with the magical fallout."

Grimacing once more as he pulled me the rest of the way to him, I sighed. "I know. But it's too late now. And I will still heal, just much slower than you did."

He wrapped his arms around me loosely, making sure not to put any pressure. His closeness helped me to relax, and I laid my head against his chest, listening to his strong heartbeat below my ear, steady and soothing.

A hundred what ifs cycled through my brain as we sat in silence. What if the spirit escaped the sanctuary? We'd never be able to find her and banish her. What if I couldn't make my wolf genes activate? Would I never regain my mark? The thought of being almost powerless after just getting a taste of what having magic was like crippled me emotionally.

It wasn't fair. What if she killed the only people I had left in my life? I might be angry at my mom, but I didn't want her to die. And I'd lose my mind if Isaiah died on me. We were just getting to know each other, but I knew I wanted him around for a long time.

He brushed his lips across the top of my head, making me shiver in a not unpleasant way.

"Let's get out of here. We need to get you home so you can rest and heal."

My stomach growled loudly.

"And eat. You need to eat. I'll make you anything you want!"

Both of us gave a little laugh as he helped me to stand, mine getting cut off by the pain of moving my body from its sitting position. I hissed as fire rippled through every muscle I had.

"Let me carry you."

He reached out to pick me up, and I shied away, once more cussing at the pain. "You're crazy. That's a long walk. I'll make it."

"Liar. And you probably weigh a hundred pounds soaking wet. Are you insulting my manly man strength?"

He curled his arm up like a weight lifter, squeezing his bicep with the opposite hand. I cut my answering laugh short when pain lanced through my ribs.

"Shit. Don't make me laugh." Closing my eyes, I drew in a slow breath, waiting for the pain to subside.

I opened them to find him right up next to me. "I'll be careful, I promise. Let me try. It will take us all day to get back to the house if you try to walk it. And you might pass out before we make it back. It's still safest within the wards, so let me get you there as quick as I can. Please?"

He took my lack of argument as agreement, and slipped his arms around me, lifting me slowly and with ease. Once settled against his chest, I had to admit it was less painful than trying to stand on my own.

"Am I hurting you?"

Having his lips so close to my own stole my breath away for a minute, and I forgot to answer him.

"Leah? I'm not hurting you, am I?"

Making an attempt to gather my wits, I shook my head. "Not nearly as much as standing on my own hurts."

"Good."

His smile melted me completely. I had to tear my

eyes away before I did something stupid. Nestling into his embrace, I closed them, listening to his heartbeat once more and trying to relax. It's not every day I went to war with an evil spirit who tried to kill me, and I was exhausted.

The next time I opened my eyes, a familiar ceiling met my gaze. The one in my room at my aunt's house. I still couldn't bring myself to think of it as my own. Not yet.

Isaiah had carried me all the way back to the house and settled me into bed while I probably hung in his arms like a limp noodle. That's a surefire way to make an impression on a guy. Hopefully my total lack of magical skills and inability to cook had endeared me to him already.

At the sound of a slight snore, I turned my head to see him sprawled in the armchair. He'd dragged it as close to the bed as he could get it and passed out in it. Disappointment that he hadn't crawled into bed beside flooded me. Before I could say anything, his eyes popped open. He must have felt me studying him, even in his sleep.

"Hey there, gorgeous. How do you feel?"

I felt my lips quirk up at the corners at his

compliment. "Not bad, considering I just had my worst day ever. And unless you hosed me off before bringing me in here, I highly doubt the word gorgeous could apply to any aspect of me."

"Well, if that remains your worst day for the rest of your life, I'd say we did alright. Wouldn't you? And all of you is gorgeous, all the time."

"Hmph. At least if my worst day is behind me, that means it can only get better from here."

He winked. "You got it."

"That chair doesn't seem like the most comfortable place for a nap."

"There weren't any other options so that I could stay close to you. I don't care for sleeping on the floor."

"Hmm... Seems to me there is a very large, perfectly good bed right here."

"It was occupied." He raised a single eyebrow at the insinuation.

"The current occupant wouldn't object to some company."

Now both brows climbed right up to his hair line. I could feel my cheeks turning pink at his surprise.

"We both need our rest. This is the most comfortable place to get it. I promise not to bite if you want to come lay down. Unless you want me to, that is."

His turn to be embarrassed by my advance made me giggle. Pulling the covers back to admit him, I scooted over toward the wall with a minimum amount of pain, and motioned him toward me. For a second he remained planted in the chair, and I wondered if I had misread some of our earlier interactions. Just as I was about to take it back, he stood up. Oh God, was he going to leave?

After another brief hesitation he sat gingerly on the edge of the bed, as if he expected the sky to come crashing down on top of him. He perched there, barely putting his weight on the mattress. Turning to look at me again, I could see him struggling as he debated the consequences of getting that close to me.

"Come on," I encouraged him, "you're letting all the heat out."

He finally stretched out next to me, pulling the blankets back over us both. For a moment he lay stiffly next to me, unmoving. Taking matters into my own hands, I pulled my pillow along and snuggled up under his arm, wordlessly demanding he make room for me, which he did. Settled in his embrace, I tilted my head up to look at him.

"Comfortable?"

He exhaled slowly and grinned. "Yeah, actually. I am."

"Good." I paused. "Thank you for everything. I don't know what I'd do without you."

"Well, luckily you aren't going to have to find out. I'm not going anywhere."

My breath hitched as his lips drifted closer to mine. "Ever?" I murmured softly.

"Uh-uh. You're stuck with me forever."

Words became superfluous as his lips brushed mine ever so gently. The tingle that began in my toes climbed through the rest of my body, pleasure replacing the last vestiges of pain. For the moment.

* * *

EPILOGUE

Unbeknownst to the two of us, as we lay recuperating, and sharing our first kiss, a young wolf from the North Eastern pack sat idly on a rock by the waterfall in the mountain. He stared into the crystal clear water, pondering life. As he did, a chill swept over him. With the ensuing shiver, his eyes bled briefly from green to icy blue before the color faded away. Blinking in confusion, he shuddered, but pushed the disconcerting feeling away.

He looked around, feeling as if he was no longer alone, but saw no one. Deep in his subconscious, the hooks were already sunk in. He had no idea that the desire to walk back and be with the pack came not from him, but an outside influence. One who would bring him nothing but torture in the days to come.

The End

* * *

Continue the StarHaven Sanctuary Series in book two, Spirit Marked, out now.

Thank you for reading the story of StarHaven Sanctuary! I cant tell you all what your support means.

As an indie author reviews are the lifeblood of our author business, as many of you know. If you enjoyed the book and feel so inclined, please leave an honest review. The QR code below will take you right to the review page!

ABOUT THE AUTHOR

Tera Lyn Cortez made the leap from voracious reader to author in 2019. In addition to books of every kind, she is a lover of coffee, the ocean, and all things chocolate.

Her home life consists of being a wife and mother to five in the lovely Pacific Northwest, although she admits to being consumed with Wanderlust. Life as a writer allows her to indulge in traveling both our world and those that live only in our imagination when she can't leave her office.

http://www.teralyncortez.com/

http://www.facebook.com/teralyncortez

ACKNOWLEDGMENTS

So many people go into the making of a book that it can be hard to keep track. In addition to my friends and family who encourage me when I'm feeling overwhelmed, I've got the professionals in my corner helping me make these books the best they can be before I send them out into the world.

For the first time I wrote this book from an outline instead of just figuring things out as I go. Thanks, Varun, for helping me with that!

Thank you to Amanda, my editor at Dark Raven Edits, for helping to whip the story into shape and making sure that we get rid of as many of those pesky typos as we can. (I know I always make plenty!)

Do you love this cover? I certainly do! Thank you to Melony at Paradise Cover Design for creating exactly what I wanted, even though I didn't know what I wanted at the time!

YOU ARE ALL AMAZING!

Made in the USA
Las Vegas, NV
10 September 2022